appeal denied

PETER CORRIS

appeal denied

A CLIFF HARDY NOVEL

ALLEN&UNWIN

Thanks to Jean Bedford, Jo Jarrah and Tom Kelly.

First published in 2007

Allen & Unwin
83 Alexander Street
Crows Nest NSW 2065
Australia
Phone: (61 2) 8425 0100
Fax: (61 2) 9906 2218
Email: info@allenandunwin.com
Web: www.allenandunwin.com

National Library of Australia
Cataloguing-in-Publication entry:

Corris, Peter, 1942– .
    Appeal denied: a Cliff Hardy novel.

    ISBN 978 174175 0 966 (pbk.).

    1. Hardy, Cliff (Fictitious character) – Fiction.
    2. Private investigators – New South Wales – Sydney –
    Fiction. I. Title.

A823.3

Set in 12/14 pt Adobe Garamond by Midland Typesetters, Australia
Printed in Australia by McPherson's Printing Group

10 9 8 7 6 5 4 3 2 1

For Lesley McFadzean

part one

1

Following my last major case, I was given a suspended sentence for various offences. This, together with an earlier serious infringement and a brief prison spell, caused the police board that handles the licensing of private enquiry agents to scrub me for life. To raise a bit of money, I handled a few minor matters before the hearing was held but that was it. I lost the appeal against their decision. The next step was an appeal to the Administrative Decisions Tribunal and I lost that one, too. Appeal denied.

'That's it, Cliff,' my solicitor, Viv Garner, said when he gave me the news. 'Unless you fancy the Supreme Court and the High Court of Australia.'

'No thanks,' I said. 'You gotta know when to fold 'em.'

'So what'll you do now? You've got no super. Your house's worth a bundle but you'll never sell it, will you?'

I shook my head. The house in Glebe was worth a lot of money, even in its rundown condition, but there were a lot of reasons why I wouldn't sell it. First, call me parochial, but I wouldn't want to live anywhere on the planet except there. Second, it held too many memories—of my first wife, Cyn, when we were young and in love, and then when we weren't; of Hilde Stoner, my ex-tenant and still a friend, now married to Frank Parker, another friend; of the women and clients and cops and enemies who'd trooped through bringing love and money and death and destruction. Too much to give up. Plus, I couldn't bear the thought of packing up all the stuff. Inertia is a powerful force.

'I'll think of something,' I told Viv. 'I had a thorough check-up from Ian Sangster the other day and he reckons I'm good for quite a few years yet.'

'Yeah, you look all right given the life you've led. Full head of hair, not much grey, not much flab. How d'you do it?'

'A pure heart. You might have to wait a bit for your cheque.'

Viv mimed shock. I shook his hand and left the house in Lilyfield from where he runs his slimmed-down business. He had heart trouble a while back and his wife monitors him closely. After the trouble I've given him over the years, I think she'd like to see me out of the picture, but Viv and I go back a long stretch. She knows that I do him good in a way, keep him in touch with the gritty stuff, and I make sure to give her my charm on full wattage.

I went for a wander around the streets with no destina-tion in mind, just to do some thinking. The appeal process had taken eight months. No income and the usual bills flowing in. Funds were low and winter was coming on— heating costs, a close-to-leaking roof to have fixed and the Falcon needed attention. At least the mortgage was cleared and my daughter Megan was in paid employment as a doctor in a hospital series on TV. Not that she'd ever been a drain because I hadn't even known about her until she was almost twenty, but there had been the odd sling and in its own way acting is as precarious a profession as private enquiry.

I think best when walking or drinking and best of all when walking towards somewhere to have a drink. I headed for a pub I knew in Victoria Road. The wind had an edge to it and I buttoned my blazer. The loss of my licence had closed doors. For years some of the big private enquiry firms had tried to recruit me and I'd knocked them back. Same story with security companies. Those lines of work were out now except, perhaps, as some sort of consultant. I didn't fancy that. It meant briefing people twenty years younger than me and writing reports—office work. In the past I'd done some casual teaching in the PEA course at a TAFE college. It wasn't a bad sideline gig—talking about old cases, bringing along the odd cop and crim to talk to the classes, scouting locations where things had gone down—but I couldn't see the TAFE people employing me again.

I got to Victoria Road where the traffic seems to get heavier from one day to the next. The walk hadn't helped, maybe a drink would. The pub was boarded up, out of business. It was happening all over the city—pubs closing down, waiting to become something else. Even Glebe had lost one, the Harold Park. Were new pubs being opened? I didn't think so. Wine bars maybe, with the beer at five bucks a middy.

Lily Truscott, my live-out lover, was waiting for me when I got back to Glebe. She knew I'd been to see Viv and pointed to the bottle I was carrying.

'Are we celebrating?'

'Not exactly, unless ridding the profession of an undesirable for good and all makes for one. Some people seem to think so.'

'I'm sorry, Cliff. That's tough.'

'I'll open this and soften the blow. Usually works.'

Lily is a freelance journalist. She rose to the top of the tree but found being an editor not as much fun as reporting. A bit like me really. So she took a pay-out and now does very well doing what she does best. She has a knack, not given to many, of making financial stories interesting. She has a house in Greenwich; I go there occasionally and she comes to my place, also occasionally. The occasions are pretty frequent.

We sat out in the pale sunshine in my tiny, badly paved courtyard where the weeds poke through and attempt to lift the bricks with a certain amount of success. We drank some wine and ate olives and cheese. It had rained the night before and water was dripping from a section of clogged guttering and rusted downpipe. Over the years, leaves and dust had built up in the guttering to provide fertile soil for a variety of botanical species.

I watched the drops for a while and poured some more wine. 'Viv's solution to the income problem is to sell the house.'

'What's his solution to the what-do-I-do-with-my-life problem?'

'He's a lawyer—he left that up to me.'

'How far have you got?'

I raised my glass. 'To here.'

'Yeah, alcoholism's a sort of career. I guess we all flirt with it.'

'I gave it a try when Cyn left me, and a few other times since. Didn't quite take.'

Lily nodded. She's been through the mill—a divorce, broken relationships, an abortion or two. She once spent a couple of weeks in Silverwater on a contempt charge for refusing to reveal a source. In a funny way our careers have run parallel. She even likes boxing and it was at the fights where her brother was on the card that I met her.

She plucked at a weed and a brick came loose. She has strong wrists. 'ASIO's recruiting,' she said. 'Intelligence, for want of a more accurate word, is a growth industry. They take on all types. You're ex-army, aren't you? What rank?'

'Second lieutenant.'

'You'd have to learn to pronounce it *lootenant*, but they might like you.'

'As Marlon Brando said to his agent when he was asked whether he'd be willing to be interviewed by Kenneth Tynan, "I'd rather be boiled in urine".'

Lily laughed. 'You could write your memoirs.'

'Boiled in urine. Tell you what, let's see if there's a film within driving distance we could stand to watch.'

There wasn't. We saw films pretty regularly and had similar tastes—political thrillers, biopics, historical stuff. We'd already seen what was on offer that appealed and the rest were animations and dumb dross. We kept promising ourselves we'd see some foreign flicks as recommended by David and Margaret, but somehow never got around to it. We had a meal in Newtown where I have an office I no longer need. Luckily, the lease is running out. We went back to my house and made love. She was gone in the morning the way she almost always is and the way I tell myself I like it—almost all the time.

Our deal is that we talk about whatever it is we're engaged on. I hadn't had much to say recently. Pursuing clients who still owed me money, keeping fit in the gym and trying not to think about the future beyond the last appeal submission don't make for interesting chat. Lily, on the other hand, always has three or four stories on the go and gives me the juicy bits. I enjoy what she says at the time but forget it pretty quickly. I usually read the published stories, or skim them.

A slightly cold morning. Coffee and the paper. No breakfast. To the gym for a forty-five minute light workout scoffed at by the gymaholics—the women with real bicep definition, the men with six-pack abs. We exchange insults in between grunts. The steam and the smell of chlorine drew me to the spa and I soaked there for a whole fifteen minute cycle, showered and got dressed feeling fit, moral and bored shitless. I was retired and very far from self-funded. Was there a support group? Did I need counselling? Any point in ringing Lawsie and complaining about a system that required private enquiry agents to wear kid gloves? I was sure I'd get a hearing.

It went on like that for a couple of days. A long overdue cheque came in and eased the pain a bit. There was still a couple of grand outstanding. Some people seem to think that being de-licensed equals no need to pay. To fend off a wave of anger and self-pity, I rang Frank Parker, retired from the New South Wales Police with the rank of deputy commissioner. Sitting pretty on his pension.

'Cliff. How's it going?'

'Ratshit, thanks, Frank. How d'you fill in the time?'

'Oh, you know. Tennis, reading, bit of volunteer work here and there.'

'Is that satisfying?'

'I spent the last years in the job in an office shuffling paper, mate. It's better than that. Time hanging heavy?'

'Yeah, and the wolf's slinking towards the door.'

'I've had you in mind. Did some web research. You can work as a PEA in the ACT without a licence. At least for now. How would you feel about Canberra?'

'Much the same as I'd feel about Hobart.'

'You know the solution. Sell the crumbling Glebe fortress to some IT couple with money coming out their arseholes. Buy a townhouse in Coogee. Learn to surf.'

'I was surfing when I was ten years old.'

'How often since then?'

'Not often.'

'There you go, learn to surf again. Or how about bush-walking? You could meet up with Bob Carr.'

'Yesterday's man. What does the new bloke do when he takes off his suit?'

'No idea. But you have to find something that you want to do, that you're good at and will bring in a buck.'

'I know. Thanks, Frank. I'll think about it.'

But I didn't have to think about it because two days later Lily was murdered.

2

The sequence of events went like this: at 10.30 am I got a telephone call.

'Mr Cliff Hardy?'

'Yes.'

'This is Detective Constable Farrow of the Northern Crimes Unit. Ms Lillian Truscott had your name in her passport as the person to contact in the event of an accident.'

That was news to me. 'She's had an accident?'

'I'm sorry to tell you, sir, that Ms Truscott is dead.'

I felt the room spin and I had to lean against the wall. I gripped the phone so hard my knuckles cracked. Lily had always been a wild driver and inclined to take risks with the breathalyser. 'A car accident?'

'No, sir.'

'What then? When?'

Constable Farrow didn't answer and I could hear muted mutterings as she shielded the phone. Then her voice came through, shakily but clear. 'Ms Truscott's body has been taken to the mortuary in Glebe. We'd be obliged if you could identify her.' Police-person Farrow sounded about twenty.

'How did she die?'

'Would you like a police car to pick you up, sir?'

'Listen, Constable, I was in the army and I've been a private investigator for longer than you've been alive. I've been around death. How did she fucking die?'

Maybe Farrow was twenty-five. Her tone hardened. 'Detective Colin Williams will meet you at the mortuary in half an hour. Thank you, Mr Hardy.'

It was just down the road. I didn't know the morgue was in Glebe when I moved there. It's an odd fact, but not many Sydney people know where it is—probably don't want to know. I was there in fifteen minutes with grief and anger raging. I parked in a no-standing zone and walked across to where a man in a suit stood near the entrance to the building. He was youngish and fit-looking with a face arranged for compassion. Maybe. He put out his hand.

'Mr Hardy?'

I ignored the hand. 'You Williams?'

He was young but he'd been in the job long enough not to take any shit. The hand dropped and the body straightened. 'DS Williams, yes.'

'How was she killed?'

I was older, greyer, unshaven, dressed sloppily, driving a beat-up car, but he was bright or experienced enough to know an angry and potentially violent man when he saw one. And he wasn't going to give any more ground than he had to. He turned away and took a step towards the entrance.

Almost over his shoulder he said, 'She was murdered. Come with me, please.'

I followed him through the heavy street doors, past a desk where he flashed his credentials and down corridors with vinyl flooring and fluorescent lights. Let's go artificial when we're dealing with the essential reality of death. I'd been here before and knew it wasn't anything like on TV, where they slot the dead into freezers and people stand around in green scrubs and white hats waiting to perform autopsies and mutter into microphones in hushed, concerned tones. Sydney doesn't have enough suspicious deaths to justify the dramatics.

Williams led me to a small, plain, antiseptic room of the sort you might go to for a blood test. A body, covered by a sheet, lay on a trolley.

'Show me,' I said.

An attendant in white overalls was standing nearby and Williams gave him a nod. He went to the trolley and pulled back the plastic sheet.

It was Lily and it wasn't Lily. The same features, hair, throat, lines and the asymmetries that make up a face. But no living face is that still, showing that the life current has been turned off. I'd seen corpses embalmed and made ready for the ground or the flames, and she didn't have that frozen, painted look. In a strange way that difference helped to give me some distance at a moment when I needed it. I nodded at Williams and stepped back.

We retraced our steps until we were outside the building again. I hadn't noticed the cold when I left my house in a shirt and jeans but I did now. I shivered as the wind hit me. Williams turned his back to the wind and lit a cigarette. He held out the packet to me and I was tempted but refused.

He took a few deep draws, exhaled and the wind carried the smoke away. 'We have to talk,' he said. 'This is your turf, Hardy. Where?'

I told him to follow me and I drove to the coffee place in Glebe Point Road next to where the Valhalla Cinema used to be. A lot of places in Glebe used to be where they aren't anymore. Too many. I found a parking spot in Hereford Street, went inside and ordered a long black. Williams must have parked well away because he took ten minutes to arrive and looked pissed off. Maybe because I hadn't ordered him a coffee. The place was thinly populated and I picked a corner furthest from the other patrons. Williams ordered at the counter and sat down. We didn't speak until the coffees arrived, mine only thirty seconds before his. Service can be slow but cops have a way of speeding it up and a savvy Glebe coffee bar worker can usually spot a cop.

Williams flipped open his notebook. 'Ms Truscott was found in her home at eight am this morning by a woman who'd come to clean. She was in her bed in an upstairs room. She'd been shot in the temple at close range.'

Lily's bedroom: upstairs like mine, sparsely furnished and untidy like mine—books by the bed, clothes on chairs, coffee mugs, baby oil, tissues … I put two spoonfuls of sugar into my coffee, stirred it and didn't say anything. I couldn't speak; the picture in my head was too stark, too wrong.

Williams sipped his flat white and then finished it in a couple of gulps, as if he needed the fuel for what he had to do. He drew in a deep breath. 'I'm going to have to get a statement from you about your relationship with Ms Truscott, about where you've been over the past twenty-four hours, and I have to take possession of the pistol registered to you as a private investigator but that you are no longer entitled to use or possess.'

'Okay,' I said.

It jolted him. 'Just okay?'

I drank some coffee and found it bitter despite the sugar. 'No, it's not okay. As of now nothing in the fucking world is okay, but I'll play along until you piss me off so much that I'll do something everybody will regret—you, me, my lawyer, everybody except the media. Understand?'

He didn't respond.

'Enjoying this, are you?' I said.

It was just a throwaway, letting-off-steam remark, but his reaction was strange, as if he'd been seriously challenged. He recovered quickly, though.

'I was told you were difficult,' he said.

The Glebe police station was only two blocks away. Williams used his mobile to get the loan of a room and recording equipment and we walked there. He lit a cigarette as soon as he closed the phone. I was glad he didn't offer me one because I might have weakened. On the walk I scarcely heard the traffic or felt the pavement under my feet. I was numb, dead to sensation. Williams had to haul me back before I stepped out against a red light into the path of a bus.

The adrenalin rush from the near-miss got my brain working again. Two women I'd loved had died early—my ex-wife Cyn of cancer, and Glen Withers, who had virtually suicided. But I hadn't been emotionally close to either of them at the time they died. This was emotionally different. I found myself calculating how long it had been since Lily and I had last made love.

Williams tugged at my arm. 'First you nearly walk into a bus, then you go catatonic. Come on.'

We crossed the road and waited for the light to cross again. I was starting to take things in. Williams was older than he looked and not a bad guy. He shot me a couple of concerned looks. He didn't swagger the way some cops do, and he didn't expect people to step out of his way. He paused to stub his cigarette on the rim of a bin and drop it in.

'You all right, Mr Hardy?' he said. 'You look cold. You should have put on a jacket.'

'I'm all right. Let's get this over with.'

I've been in the Glebe police station quite a few times, never for drinks and nibbles. It's been tarted up more than once over the years, but something of its essence always comes back—a look, smell and feel that speak of long hours, tiredness, loss, anger, frustration and takeaway food. Williams spoke to the woman at the desk and we were shown up a set of stairs to an interview room.

'Water?' Williams said.

I nodded. He went out and came back with two plastic cups. He'd done this before and more times than me: he set up the video, adjusted the focus and the angle and we got down to it.

'Detective Sergeant Colin Williams, Northern Crimes Unit, card number W781, interviewing Mr Cliff Hardy at Glebe police station.' He glanced at his watch and announced the time and date.

I identified myself, said I'd waived the right to have a solicitor present, and that I'd known Lillian Truscott for a little over two years. I said that we didn't live together but spent a lot of time in each other's company. I said that we'd taken a couple of short holidays together—to Byron Bay and North Queensland—and that I'd last seen her three nights before when she'd stayed at my place. I said that I'd spent time in my Newtown office in the afternoon of the previous day, had then driven home and from there walked to the Toxteth Hotel where I'd had a few drinks and played pool with my regular pool partner, Daphne Rowley. I went home, heated up some leftovers, watched television, read a book and went to bed.

Williams was watching me and listening intently. He was confident that the equipment was working. I kept my head up and didn't fidget.

I said, 'This morning I read the paper, did the cross-word, drank coffee and then Constable Farrow called me. Following that, I met DS Williams at the Glebe mortuary.'

I sipped some water and stopped talking.

'That's it?'

'That's my statement. Oh, the pistol's at home under lock and key. You can come by and collect it.'

'I will, but first I'd like to ask you some questions.'

'Ask. I'll consider whether to answer.'

'You've said when you last saw Ms Truscott. When did you last contact her?'

'The night before last. We spoke on the phone.'

'Planning to meet when?'

'No plan, we played it by ear.'

'It seems a very loose relationship.'

'Think what you like.'

'Ms Truscott was a journalist. Do you know what she was working on?'

'Financial stories.'

'Specifically?'

'I don't know. You'll have to check her computer, if it's still there.'

'Do you have any reason to think it's not?'

My patience was running out. 'Use your head.'

'Speaking of finance, you've been barred as a private investigator. How are you making a living?'

I drank some more water and sucked in a sour breath. 'I'm not. I'm living on savings and trying to call in some unpaid debts.'

'Did you and Ms Truscott ever quarrel?'

'Yes.'

'What about?'

'She thought Anthony Mundine had a future. I wasn't so sure.'

I made a cutting motion and folded my arms. Williams turned off the video.

'That doesn't leave the best impression,' he said.

'I don't give a shit. I'll talk to you off the record if you'll answer some questions for me.'

He shook his head. 'No.'

I stood up. 'That's it then. Pop your cassette and we'll get the gun. That's if I can remember where it is.'

'You'd better.'

I let him have the last word. He had the body language of a man preoccupied with something other than what he was doing. Two preoccupied men together.

3

Williams followed me in his red Camry. He didn't look too impressed with my house. Most don't, unless they're thinking *potential*. I gave him the .38 and he put it in a paper bag. Contrary to what people see on television, evidence bags are not made out of plastic. This isn't environmentalism, just a matter of reducing the risk of contamination.

As he was leaving, Williams said, 'Why did you waive the right to a lawyer?'

'I've caused mine enough trouble lately and run up more than enough expense for myself. I'll swim along solo until I get out of my depth.'

'You're not what I expected.'

'What did you expect?'

With his hand on the front gate, he allowed himself a thin smile. 'I said I wouldn't answer any questions. I hope you're not going to mount some sort of vigilante action on this, Mr Hardy.'

'No chance of that, if you catch and convict the person responsible.'

'We'll do our best. We may need your … further help.'
He handed me his card.

'Sergeant, that's a two-way street.'

Later that day Tony Truscott, Lily's boxing brother, who was a good deal younger than her, rang me.

'Cliff, I just got back from Fiji and got the message on my phone. Jesus, how could this happen?'

'I don't know, Tony. They were on to me because she'd put my name in her passport as the one to contact, you being out of the country so often and all that.'

'Yeah, yeah. Jesus, Lily …'

'I identified her and I gave a statement to the cops. What're they asking you to do?'

'Nothing. They say they're doing a fucking autopsy. Jesus …'

'That's standard, mate. All I know is that she was shot at close range, probably when she was asleep. It doesn't help, but … you know.'

'I dunno what to do.'

'Because your mother and father are dead and there's no other siblings or kids involved, you'd be next of kin. They'll want you to make funeral arrangements when the … her body's released. Are you up for that?'

'Fuck, no.'

'Anyone with you who's had some experience?'

'Jerry Hawkins, I guess—my manager.'

'Get him to make the calls—to the police and then to a funeral place. There'll have to be a notice in the papers. She had a lot of friends, Tony. They'll want to show up and you'll have to arrange a thing for afterwards.

Can Jerry organise all that? Did he know her?'

'Yeah. He'll do it.'

'Give him my number and tell him I'll help any way I can.'

'Okay. Thanks, Cliff. You all right?'

'No. She wouldn't want any religion and she'd want a party. Can you make that clear to Jerry?'

'Yeah.'

'Tell him I want to say a few words. How about you?'

He was crying and I was close.

'I'll … I'll try. Jesus, Lily.'

Lily was cremated at Rookwood. The ceremony, conducted by one of the writers she'd worked closely with on a Fairfax paper, Tim Arthur, went as she'd have wished—no bullshit, good jokes. Arthur did the honours well. He talked about the stories he and Lily had worked on together, and the couple of Walkley Awards they'd won. He said she'd deserved them more than him but he'd accepted just the same. Struck the right note. I spoke briefly, along with some friends and colleagues. Tony managed a halting, distressed sentence or two that didn't help the rest of us keep our composure.

The wake was at Tony's place in Hunters Hill—a sprawling sandstone affair he'd bought with his winnings. Tony was doing pretty well as a world-ranked welterweight contender, fighting mostly in the US. I remembered that he'd got on the web when he'd paid his deposit on the place, and checked the history of the area.

'Bet some of the nobs think it's named after that governor bloke, the one who had the stoush with Macarthur over the rum and that.'

Lily and I were having a celebratory drink with him at the time. 'I thought that was Bligh,' I said.

Tony shook his head. 'This Hunter bloke, too. Well, turns out it isn't. It's named after some farm in Scotland, so up theirs.'

Tony had been nervous about moving into such an up-market neighbourhood, but it had worked out all right. His house was one of the old ones designed by 'some French-man', he told us. Apparently Italian craftsmen had worked on it and that showed. When the neighbours saw that Tony was spending money on restoration rather than renovation, they accepted him.

The day of the wake was cool and fine and the party took place mainly on the big upstairs deck that looked out over the Parramatta River. Jerry Hawkins had arranged the catering and there were masses of finger food and a flood of booze for the eighty-odd people attending. Lily's favourite blues records—BB King, Howling Wolf, Muddy Waters, John Lee Hooker—were playing and the only thing wrong with the party was that Lily wasn't there. She'd have liked it.

Two years and a bit with someone, especially the way we played it, isn't long enough to get to know all a partner's friends and a lot of the people there didn't have a clue who I was until someone filled them in. I caught some curious glances and I could imagine the conversations.

That's her bloke.

What does he do?

He's a private eye, or was until he got rubbed out.

Are the cops looking at him?

You'd reckon, wouldn't you?

Tony introduced me to Jerry and I thanked him for the good job he'd done. Tony was on orange juice—unless he'd spiked it. Who could blame him? He was about twelve years younger than his sister—'an afterthought' as she called him, and he'd looked up to her from day one. Their mother was a frustrated writer. She'd approved of Lily's chosen profession. The father was a truckie who'd built up a middle-sized business. Tony was all the late-life son he could've asked for. According to Lily, they'd been a successful family until cancer got her mother in her mid-fifties and her father, at sixty-odd, a few years later. It was one of the reasons Lily hadn't wanted children.

With too many of these memories on my mind, I talked briefly to a few people I knew, but basically wanted to be on my own and let this 'celebration of Lily's life' go on around me. I walked to the deck rail and looked out over the water. There was a good breeze and the boats were making the most of it. It's not something I ever took to. The few times I tried, it seemed to consist of alternating between being bored rigid and working your arse off while someone yelled at you. I guess if you did it long enough to know what you were about and had enough money, you could get to do the yelling.

I'd had a big scotch on arrival and a glass of wine since, or was it two? I finished the drink, whatever number it was, and thought about another. Against that, if I ate a few sandwiches and had some coffee and took a walk around the streets, it'd probably be safe to drive home. Home—not a lot to feel good about there. I was leaning towards another drink or two and a taxi, when a man appeared beside me.

'Cliff Hardy?'

'Yes.'

A small boat about to tip over in the wind caught my eye and I watched it without looking at the man who'd spoken. Rude of me, but for the first time in a while I was looking at some outside action, instead of in at myself.

'I'm Lee Townsend.'

That got my attention. 'I'm sorry,' I said. 'I was miles away.'

I recognised him. Townsend was an investigative print and television reporter, the sort that get up the noses of politicians, bureaucrats and business types—my kind of guy. He'd broken big stories on police corruption, political cover-ups and government department mismanagement. He'd fronted several television documentaries that had made his image as well known as his written work. He had a couple of spin-off books to his credit that I hadn't read.

I was facing him now, using the word loosely. He stood about 160 centimetres at the most and his build would have to be described as puny. The magic of television had concealed this.

He saw my reaction. 'Yeah, I know,' he said. 'People think I'm a six-footer like you.'

I shook his hand. 'Jean-Paul Sartre was one fifty-eight centimetres on his best days,' I said.

He laughed. 'Thank you for that. Your eulogy was good. Spot on.'

'You knew Lily?'

'A bit in the early days when we were wage slaves. She had the handicap of being a woman, and I was too fucking small to be taken seriously.'

'You both did okay.'

He placed his glass on the balcony rail. Looked like scotch. He wore an expensive lightweight suit. I was in a dark blazer and dark pants, blue shirt—closest I could get

to the suit look. No tie. Lily said ties were as stupid as gloves
and she was right.

'I'd like to have a talk with you,' Townsend said. 'Here,
if you're agreeable, or later if you'd prefer it.'

He might have looked different from his TV persona
but his strong, resonant, convincing voice was the same.
I had a feeling he'd be worth talking to. In a strange way he
reminded me of Lily—smaller, of course.

'Now'd be good,' I said. 'Lately I've been talking mostly
to myself. What about a drink? Was that scotch?'

He nodded. I picked up his glass and mine and headed
for the bar. The crowd had thinned out a bit but not
much. You can count on journos to form a good, solid
hard core at any boozy bash. They've always got plenty to
talk about and it takes a long while for the grog to make
them boring.

Muddy was doing his number: Lily and I had seen the
movie of the Band's supposed last performance—*The Last
Waltz*—before they kept reincarnating. Muddy had done
the song in his suit, but still managed to look as if he was
down on the delta:

Ain't that a man?

Ain't that a man, child?

I did some handshaking and nodding on the way
to the bar. I ate a couple of ham and cheese sandwiches
while I waited to name my poison. I got my hands
around two scotches large enough to sustain a decent talk
and went back out onto the deck. Townsend was still
there and on his own. I finished half my drink before
I even got there. With the first drink and the wines—
probably three if I was honest—on board and the
emotional drag, the whisky hit me. I was suddenly

conscious of the need to walk carefully and watch where I was going.

I put his drink on the rail. 'What's on your mind?'

'It's a week since Lily was killed. What are your sources telling you about the police investigation?'

'I don't have any sources. The few I had don't want to know me since I got scrubbed. I did have a particular bloke who—'

'Frank Parker.'

'Yeah, but Frank's got other fish to fry. Plus he's called in a lot of favours over the years, some of them for me. I'd say he's just about tapped out. Why?'

'Don't you want to know who killed her and why?'

'I don't give a shit about why.'

'Understood. Well. I *have* got a police source and what I'm told makes me want to look into Lily's death as closely as I can.'

'What does he tell you?'

Townsend picked up his glass, rattled the ice and took a drink. 'Just a minute. You're making assumptions. Two things. I'm after a story of course, but I liked Lily. She never put me down for being a short-arse and I admired her work. And did I say my source was a male?'

A smartie. I was a bit drunk and a bit annoyed. 'Okay, okay. You liked Lily and some cop's been blabbing to you. So what?'

'We're getting off on the wrong foot here.'

'I'm a bit pissed.'

'Not surprising. Why don't we leave it till tomorrow.'

I was about to grab him when I realised how silly it'd look. I was twenty-plus centimetres taller and would've outweighed him by twenty kilos. He stood his ground.

'I'd rather talk now,' I said. 'Please.'

Townsend glanced around to make sure there was no one within earshot. 'As you'd expect, the police took away her computers—desktop and laptop—and two thumb drives. I'm told they were wiped clean beyond any point of data recovery. That brought the detectives to a full stop. Their only working theory was that Lily was killed because of something she was writing, or was going to write.'

'That's logical. She'd brought down some high-fliers.'

'Sure, but I think there're holes in the story. Why wouldn't the killer just take the computer stuff? How likely is it that the person who shot her had the IT skills to clean the drives?'

'An accomplice?'

'Which means a witness. Remember she was shot with a .22—that's a professional job, as you'd know. How many professional killers are happy to have some computer nerd hanging around the workplace?'

I could see his point. And Lily's work station was on the glassed-in balcony attached to her bedroom. She liked to be able to jump out of bed and go straight to the keyboard when an idea struck her. I knew that when she'd had the house rebuilt after a fire had destroyed the previous one, she hadn't wanted any doors between the bedroom and the balcony. A friend had talked about *feng shui* and I could remember Lily's response.

'Bullshit,' she'd said. 'Breezes and access.'

I told Townsend about the layout. 'Even assuming that the computer guy came in after Lily was killed, he'd have to be working for some time in full view of her.'

'I can't see it, can you?' Townsend said. 'A computer whiz who's that much of a hard case?'

I shrugged. 'It's possible. They let them play with computers in jail. And they reckon some of the game players are
so desensitised to violence that they could play while their
mothers' throats were being cut.'

'D'you believe that, Hardy?'

'No. So what do you think happened?'

'I told you I have a police source. It's all a bit vague at
the moment, but my suspicion, based on the little I've been
told, is that the police cleaned the decks.'

4

'You've got me confused,' I said. 'The police're covering up a murder. Why?'

'I told you before the *why* was important.'

'I'm trying to follow you. Lily was killed because of something she was writing that involved police?'

'Perhaps, perhaps not. It wasn't her area, was it? More likely some dirty business deal.'

'Comes back to the same question—what's the police motive for a cover-up?'

'Raises interesting possibilities, doesn't it? Say the detective looks through Lily's stuff and sees he can go in for some blackmail for the big bucks on the basis of what she's written. Say he's got gambling debts, say he's being black-mailed himself for something else.'

I hadn't finished the drink and was sucking in some of the rapidly cooling fresh air. Scepticism was setting in. 'You're a conspiracy theorist.'

'Have to be. The blank drives need explaining. The killer wants to eliminate Lily. Not worried about what she's writing. The cop sees possibilities in what she's writing. He doesn't care about who killed her. What's one unsolved murder more or less? He gets the police IT guy onside.

They copy the incriminating material and cook up the story about everything being wiped. Who's going to contradict them? Look, it's speculation, I admit, but I really think police are involved—criminally. Of course, I could be quite wrong. I'll have to work harder on my police informant.'

He'd finished his drink and was standing there, all 160 centimetres of him, in his neat suit. I decided I didn't like him much.

'Tell me this,' I said. 'Is your main interest in who killed Lily, or in your theoretical blackmailing cop?'

'And in what he had to sell, you should add.'

Still the smartarse. 'Consider it added.'

'I'm interested in all of it, Mr Hardy, but it's complicated and dangerous and difficult. That's why I need your help.'

I thought about the proposition as I stood there with the party going on noisily behind me and the boats below starting to head for home as dark clouds gathered overhead and the wind sprang up. Lily had advised Tony against building a McMansion somewhere and recommended buying this place instead. We were here because of her in two ways and I was missing her in every way. Finding who had killed her wouldn't bring her back of course, but looking would keep me in touch with her in a way, while doing what I did best.

'You've got my interest,' I said.

'Good. When you think about it, apart from the stuff I've told you, is there anything that strikes you as odd about the police behaviour to date?'

'Yeah. I can account for my movements in the early part of the night but not after that. I thought they might have been a bit tougher on me.'

'You had someone to alibi you? Did they question him?'

'Her. A woman I play pool with at my local. I don't know. I just assumed it.'

'That's one starting point, then. You should ask her if they got onto her and how hard they pushed.'

'Okay. What other starting points are there?'

'The senior investigator, Inspector Vincent Gregory. Your mate Parker should be able to tell you something about him.'

'What about your informant of undisclosed gender?'

'I'm sorry about that. Must've sounded like a prick. I didn't know how much to tell you until I got your reaction. It's a woman, Constable Jane Farrow—very junior, very concerned.'

'Why's she talking to you?'

'D'you want another drink?'

'No. C'mon, let's get this straight.'

'I met her at a party three weeks ago. Turns out she likes small men. Gregory is also a small man and she liked him, too. Not as much as before.'

'Before you?'

'Yeah, but more so since the investigation into Lily's murder.'

The light dropped as the clouds moved west and blocked out the weakening rays of the sun. In a way, against what I'd been feeling just before this latest titbit of information, I wanted to get clear of Townsend, the house, the city, the country if need be. Use up some frequent flier points and get as far away as ... where? Norfolk Island? Lord Howe? Wouldn't help.

'Has she told you who the IT guy is?'

'No, but she might.'

'What happened to DS Williams? I thought he was in charge. He's the one who talked to me initially.'

'Apparently he's out of the picture. There's your next starting point.'

I still didn't like his one-upping style. He was dedicated but quite what to was hard to say. I agreed to work with him as best I could—finding out about Gregory, having a talk to Williams, while he got what he could from Constable Farrow. We exchanged numbers and agreed to stay in touch. I was sure he was holding something back but so was I. Lily had used my computer from time to time, and recently. And she'd always carried a thumb drive with her.

I had a few words with various people as I made my way out and found Tony sitting by himself, staring at his orange juice. He was stone cold sober, so the drink was exactly what it seemed.

'She was so good to me, Cliff. Always there, even when I was doing fucking stupid things.'

'I know.'

'I can't believe she's gone. It just doesn't seem right.'

'It isn't.'

'I've been thinking. You're a detective, right? I've phoned the cops a couple of times but they don't tell me anything. Maybe you can find out ...'

'I'm on it already, Tony. I'll let you know how it goes and I know I can call on you if I need any help.'

He nodded. 'Yeah. You bet.'

The party was winding down but a mob of stayers was settling in. Coffee was being served and I stopped to get some and eat two more sandwiches, thinking that after a bit of a walk I'd be okay to drive. As I was finishing the coffee a middle-aged man approached me.

'Mr Hardy, I'm Patrick Henke.'

We shook hands. 'I seem to know the name,' I said.

'Ms Truscott's solicitor.'

'Right.'

'This is a terrible thing, terrible. Such a … such a very able woman.'

'Yes, well …'

'She mentioned you a few times over the past couple of years as I handled some things for her. I'll be sending you a formal letter, but since you're here it seems appropriate to tell you now. Ms Truscott's will divides her estate, which consists of a considerable number of very solid shares and her house in Greenwich, between her brother Anthony and yourself.'

I walked the Hunters Hill streets for over an hour without knowing where I was or where I was going. I was stunned by what Henke had told me. It made me rethink my relationship with Lily. It had seemed to me to be equally loose and open-ended on both sides. But perhaps it wasn't. I'd never given a thought to leaving anything in my will to anyone other than my daughter Megan. All it'd amount to was the Glebe house. That was worth a fair amount even in its neglected state, but I wasn't planning to shuffle off for quite some time. Lily would have thought the same, but she'd made a different decision.

I wondered if Henke had told Tony. Probably not, given Tony's fragile state. I wondered how he'd take it.

Why hadn't she told me? Was she waiting for me to say something along the lines of putting our relationship on a different footing? It made me wish we'd talked more about 'us', something we almost never did, as if we were both afraid that to talk about it would spoil it. And now it was spoilt well and truly. Again, I felt guilty: I hadn't paid proper attention to her work, and now it seemed I hadn't paid proper attention to her feelings.

But one thing was for sure: licence or no licence, I was going to give the investigation into who killed her everything I had.

5

I got home late, tired and depressed. There were a few messages on the answering machine—one from the bank about my MasterCard, a couple of condolences. Hilde Stoner had rung to apologise for Frank and her not making it to the funeral. They liked Lily a lot and had wanted to be there, but there was some kind of crisis with their son Peter, who was aid-working in Asia with his wife and their infant twin girls. Hilde and Frank were waiting on a phone call. Understandable.

I went upstairs, looked at the computer but couldn't find the motivation to turn it on. Not now. I opened the wardrobe in the room that doubles as a study and guest bedroom and saw some of Lily's clothes—a couple of pairs of pants, a blouse, a dress, a jacket. Her toothbrush and a few bits of makeup were in the upstairs bathroom. There'd be a few of her books lying around. I'd be willing to bet I'd find a pair of shoes kicked under a chair. Probably some knickers and tights in the dirty clothes basket.

I was overseas in the army fighting for freedom when my mother died. My sister told me later how disposing of her clothes and other things had broken my father up, even though they'd been at odds with each other for decades. Different in every way. It'd be the work of a few minutes for me, but I had some idea now of how he must have felt. The emptiness was making me think back further than I cared to go. Filling in the spaces. It'd been a strange household to grow up in, requiring deception and negotiation between the parents every step of the way. Perhaps it had stood me in good stead for my profession.

I drank some wine and didn't taste it. I had no appetite. Lily had given me a book for my birthday—*1001 Movies You Must See Before You Die.* I sat with it on my lap, turning over the pages, looking at the pictures. It helped: I thought about some of the films—*Casablanca, The Magnificent Seven, The Third Man, Rocco and His Brothers, Chariots of Fire, Manhattan*—and the images took me away from where I was and what would never happen again with Lily and what I was going to do next.

Eventually, the tiredness became terminal, but, after the day's events, I was afraid of dreams and disturbances. My most recent injury—of many—had been a badly sprained ankle when I'd attempted a triple jump, something at which I'd once been a good performer, on the sand at Byron Bay. Showing off for Lily. The ligaments were damaged and the ankle hurt like hell for a couple of weeks. Ian Sangster had prescribed some sleeping pills, which I'd taken for as long as I'd needed to. Now I found a few left over in their foil in the bathroom cupboard and took one with a light scotch and soda. I tidied up a bit, erased the phone messages, put the movie book on the shelves and made it up the stairs to bed. Just.

*

Hilde rang in the morning to say that the crisis for Peter and his family in Bangladesh was over.

'Good news,' I said.

'How are you making out, Cliff?'

'I'm okay. I need to speak to Frank. Is he around?'

Frank came on the line. I said, 'What can you tell me about Vincent Gregory?'

'What do you need to know and why?'

'I'm looking into Lily's murder.'

'You've got no standing, mate.'

'You think I care about that? Anyway, I'm working with someone who has got standing.'

That was stretching it, but at least it got past Frank's first objection. He was silent for a while. Once a cop, always a cop. Frank hadn't exactly been squeaky clean for the whole of his time in the force. Back in the seventies it was almost impossible to avoid a bit of this and a bit of that. Do a Nelson. Turn a blind eye, go with the flow, set a thief to catch a thief. Frank had never taken a dollar and he despised those who did, but there was still that thing called the police culture. In the past, Frank had given me information about ex-cops, some of whom had gravitated to my profession, but Gregory was a serving officer and Frank knew what pressures that implied.

'You'd better tell me what you've got and maybe I can contribute something.'

'I'll have to think about that. Thanks. I'll get back to you.'

'Hey, Cliff—come on …'

'Listen. Lily left me half of what she's worth. That's a lot and I never gave a thought to doing the same. I feel ratshit about that on top of everything else, and I reckon the police investigation's a dud. I don't give a flying fuck about Inspector Gregory's reputation or his future or the New South Wales Police Service in general. Why should I? They scrubbed me for doing my job. I'll find out some other way.'

I hung up on my best friend.

I had to get out of the house. I drove to the Redgum gym in Leichhardt and threw myself into a workout routine much more severe than usual—double sets on the machines, longer on the treadmill. I worked up a sweat and stuck at the free weights until I reached 'fail'—when you can't do another lift—something I usually avoid like the plague. Wesley Scott, the West Indian proprietor and trainer, gave me a massage. Deep tissue. Hurt like hell.

'You're strung tight, man,' he said. 'What's troubling you?'

I told him with as few details as possible.

'That's tough. So you think putting yourself through this kinda pain is going to help?'

'I'll tell you something, Wes,' I said as I rolled off the table. 'I'm going to put some bugger through pain, no mistake.'

I showered and went home, denying myself the usual after-workout coffee in the Bar Napoli a few doors away. The activity had done me good. I went straight to the computer and began to look for Lily's files. I didn't find any current ones, just a couple of incomplete drafts of stories already published.

Lily could be secretive about her work, one of the reasons I never questioned her too closely. Had she been more so lately? I couldn't remember. I got up and opened the wardrobe, thinking I'd better do something about the clothes. St Vincent de Paul seemed the best bet—Lily hadn't gone in for Donna Karan power dressing. I took out the hanger holding the jacket and prepared to drop it over the back of the typing chair while I reached in for the next hanger. Something fell out of the jacket pocket—a packet of cigarettes. Like me, Lily had given up smoking years before. I hung the jacket back up, retrieved the packet from the floor and opened it. Hard pack. Twenty-three king size filter cigarettes. Two missing. Had she taken to the fags on the q.t.? I doubted it. But then I didn't know she'd put me in her will.

The packet felt funny. I'd lapsed myself once or twice and had also bought them often enough for informants to know what they felt like, even though my own preference had been for rollies. I took the packet to the desk and shook it. Twenty-three cigarettes about two-thirds of their true length came out, then a layer of foil. Wedged in the bottom of the packet was a thumb drive.

Lily's files were a chaos of notes, interview transcripts, downloaded material and draft paragraphs. How she honed them into the clear, insightful stories she produced was a mystery. The stuff bore her unmistakable imprint—frequent swearwords, wry asides and capitals for emphasis, the way she'd written in notes left for me and in her emails and postcards. I made a pot of coffee and sat down to work out what she'd been doing. One thing was clear: she'd kept a running record of the dates of the writing and research in reference to the deadlines she entered at the top of the files. This was all very recent work.

As always, Lily had been working on several stories at once. There appeared to be three—a piece about money laundering by a media personality, an investigation of a political figure suspected of running interference with the immigration authorities for a mate in the sex-slave business, and a publisher with a couple of current best-seller non-fiction books on his list, but no royalties paid to the writers or wages to his staff or the printers, and the publisher nowhere to be found.

I scratched the last one as being of interest only to the chattering classes and unlikely to involve the police, whose interest in literature is limited to say the least. The other two stories had distinct possibilities of a police connection. I scrolled through them, making notes on the dates, initials and financial details. Lily had told me that she used initials in the early stages of her investigations, partly for security purposes, partly because it amused her. She also said that she reversed and scrambled the initials which could be unscrambled by a key known only to herself. I'd laughed at her and told her she was bullshitting. She hadn't contradicted me, but she'd winked and called me a naive gumshoe.

So I was left with two investigations of serious crimes and a jumble of initials which might relate directly to the people involved or might not. Probably not. The image of Lily winking came back to me in full force. She'd meant it. I dealt mostly with the obvious, she plumbed some dodgy depths. I copied the notes and the two files onto a disk and tried to see if Lily had accessed any emails via my computer. I knew her address and logged on. Nothing. *Careful Lily*, I thought, *but you protected your work better than yourself, and I wasn't there* ...

I'd drunk three cups of strong black coffee and was a bit wired. I took the disk out of the computer and put it on the desk with the thumb drive. I was buzzing, connecting, jumping ahead of myself. There was an obvious way to flush out Lily's killer, if it had anything to do with what she'd been working on—it had to have, didn't it?—and that was to let whoever was interested know that I had the incriminating material. Was I up for that? Yes, I was, but how to do it?

Lily hadn't neglected security. She'd installed a sophisticated alarm system in her house which had either been bypassed or she'd forgotten to activate it. Not unknown. Whoever I was up against now was good at whatever he, or she, or they, did. But so was I.

6

I phoned Daphne Rowley to ask her if the cops had checked on my alibi for the early part of the night of Lily's death.

'Just now,' she said.

'How d'you mean?'

'This D got me on the phone and then came around. Had a policewoman with him.' She gave an amused snort. 'For protection, I guess.'

'That'd be Gregory, would it?'

'No. Hang on, I've got his card here … hard-nut wog named Kristos.'

Nothing politically correct about Daphne. 'Came on strong, did he?'

'I'll say. He wanted to know the exact time you arrived and when you left. How many games we played, how long we held the table. The lot.'

'What did you tell him?'

'What I could remember. Who keeps track of time when the balls are clicking, if you'll excuse the expression, and the schooners're going down?'

'Right. Did he take notes?'

'You kidding? He left that to the sheila and her Palm Pilot—Constable What's-her-face.'

'Farrow?'

'That's it. She seemed okay, for a copper.'

I thanked her and rang off. Here was a new player and a new level of interest, and I wondered why. I got the answer within a few minutes when Tony Truscott appeared at my door. He was wearing sweats and said he'd been doing some jogging.

'From Hunters Hill?'

'Fuck, no. Around your Jubilee Park here. Lily ... told me about it. Jogging's so fucking boring you need to have something to look at. I like the water and the birds and the trees and the bridge, you know.'

'Yeah. Coming in, Tony?'

'No, mate, I have to be at the gym in half an hour. It was a good bash for Lily, wasn't it?'

'Sure was. So ...?'

Like most boxers, Tony had trouble keeping still. It was fatal to do so in the ring, and the habit carried over into everyday life. He swayed and jiggled, just a little. 'I heard from Lily's solicitor about her will. Just wanted you to know, man, that it's cool with me. You were good for her.'

'Thanks, Tony. I dunno ... it broke me up a bit.'

'Yeah, well, the thing is, this fucking copper came around trying to make a big thing of it.'

'Detective named Kristos?'

'Yeah, you know him?'

In a strange way I felt I did, even though it was only the second time the name had come up. I'd met them before—middle-ranked officers aspiring to climb higher in the eyes of their loftier bosses.

'Heard of him,' I said. 'What did he have to say?'

'Wanted to know all about you, but his fucking meaning was clear—reckoned you could've killed Lily for the money.'

'What did you say, or do?'

Tony was really jiggling now. 'Jerry would've been proud of me. I wanted to hit him, first off. Then I wanted to tell him to go fuck himself. But I just told him to leave my home.'

I had to smile. The expression was so unlike Tony, I could imagine the control it had taken to produce it.

'What did he do?'

'What could he do? He's a big bastard who looked like he'd have a go if I'd been willing. He had this sexy police-woman with him and didn't want to look a wuss. But off he went. He's bad news, Cliff. If you need some help ...'

'Like I said before, I'll ask. Thanks, Tony. Go and sweat some more.'

He turned and moved down the path to the gate. He threw a punch at an overgrown bush, maybe a weed. 'Are you ...?'

'I'm on it, mate. However long it takes.'

He nodded and threw a combination. 'I'm moving up. The WBA title's vacant. I could be in for a shot. Next one's for Lily, Cliff.'

'God help him,' I said.

All I had to work with were Lily's encrypted initials. I remembered Tim Arthur, at the wake, saying how closely he and Lily had worked on some stories. Would he know about her code? Arthur had retired in his mid-fifties as an editor, presumably on a big pay-out, but he wrote an occasional column for *Blackstone*, a magazine dealing with legal matters. I called the magazine and got a phone number for Arthur. I rang him and he agreed to meet me. He was due to play golf at Moore Park at midday but he said he'd get there an hour early for some practice and I could talk to him then.

The sky was leaden with rain threatening, but golfers will play any time except when there's lightning and thunder. It was cold, too. I rugged up and drove to the course. It was mid-week and the car park was full, evidently a competition day. I squeezed into a spot between two 4WDs. The youngster in the pro shop told me that I'd find Arthur in the second bay at the driving range.

It was a massive concrete and steel structure with a roof and about thirty spots for the golfers to hit balls down into an area of a couple of acres. A machine to scoop the balls up was parked at the end of the range and when I arrived there were twenty or more devotees hitting, cursing, hitting again. Arthur was a tall, rangy bloke, still thin in his early sixties, and to my ignorant eye he seemed to have a smooth stroke. I watched him hit six or seven balls a very long way and couldn't see why he needed to practise.

He caught sight of me and gestured for me to wait. He put the club he'd been using back in his bag, selected another and hit again. This time the balls didn't go nearly as far but they described pretty, looping arcs and Arthur seemed satisfied. He put the club back, left the ball bucket that was almost empty where it was, and wheeled his buggy towards me. The others were still hitting and Arthur put his finger to his lips and led the way out of earshot.

We'd met once or twice before the wake and only briefly then. We shook hands.

'Did you want to have a hit? You look like you've got the build.'

'No, thanks. I'm a golf virgin and think I'll stay that way. You looked good. What's your handicap?'

'Nine. Used to be four. Age adds the strokes. What's on your mind, Cliff? Has to be Lily.'

According to the signs, we were walking towards the first tee. I told him I was unsatisfied with the police investigation and was following up some lines of enquiry of my own. I said Lily had been working on some stories and I had drafts and notes and thought they might have a bearing on her murder.

'Possibly,' he said. 'She was a goer. We both got death threats when we were working on an immigration scam story. How can I help you?'

We reached the tee and sat down. A group of players were hitting and there were two other groups of four standing by. Arthur's companions hadn't yet arrived so I had time. A voice over the PA system told the next group to hit. I took my notebook from my pocket and showed him the list of initials that had been sprinkled through Lily's notes.

'Can you make any sense of these? Did Lily let you in on her codes when you were working together?'

He nodded. 'A bit. Let's have a look.'

I handed him the sheet and he scanned it. 'Let's see, yes—POW, that means police officer, don't ask me why. BW stands for bureaucrat of some kind; SB means politician. I assume it stands for scumbag. I don't recognise the others. Oh, yeah, VER indicates a clergyman.'

'Rev, reversed.'

'You got it.'

The next group was called up. They completed their practice swings and lined up.

'What about the initials, sometimes two, sometimes three or four. They have to be names, right?'

'Yes, but she scrambled them just as it suited her. So that HJW could be John Winston Howard or William Henry Jones. She knew what she meant. That's about as much as I can tell you.'

I already knew about the scrambled name initials, but he was trying to be helpful and I thanked him.

We sat in silence watching the next group hit off. Four players, two groans, two calls of 'Great shot' and they were away. I saw Arthur signal to a new arrival. I didn't have him for much longer and I racked my brains to think if there was anything more to get from him.

'I'm working on the theory that something Lily was currently working on led to her death,' I said. 'But you mentioned death threats in the past. Does anything strike you as a long-term possibility? Someone with a standing grievance?'

'I'd have to think about that. We stepped on quite a few toes, Lily and I. A few people went to jail and there was at least one suicide. I'd have to get back to you after I refresh my memory at home.'

He took a glove from his pocket, pulled it on and flexed his fingers. Another salute to a member of his group. I gave him my card with the mobile number and email address. He looked at it before putting it carefully in his shirt pocket.

Arthur's group was called up.

'You lost your licence, didn't you?'

'Yeah.'

'Thin ice.'

'Don't I know it.'

He opened the seat on his buggy and took out a ball and other bits and pieces. I guessed this was what semi-retirement was all about—finding ways to fill in the days. For the first time I thought about Lily's legacy in terms of the security it'd give me. I could probably retire, but, putting aside that I'd already been forcibly retired in theory, I didn't fancy it. I didn't play golf and I didn't fish. You can only go to the gym so often, travel so much, read so many books, listen to so much music, see so many films.

Arthur moved off and suddenly turned back. 'Didn't I see you talking to Lee Townsend at the wake?'

I nodded.

'What did you make of him?'

'Hard to say.'

'I wouldn't trust that little prick as far as I could throw him, which would be a fair way in the right mood. I'll be in touch.'

7

That was a turn-up. I'd been thinking of taking my meagre evidence about Lily's work to Townsend and mulling it over with him. Now I wasn't so sure. Arthur was the last man in his group to tee off and he hit what looked like a solid shot to me and drew appreciative noises from the others. He gave me a wave as he went down the fairway. Not the time to question him about what he meant.

The rain held off, though I didn't like their chances of getting through the whole game dry. But then, the game originated in Scotland, so what could they expect? They had big umbrellas and waterproof gear so they'd survive. The threat of rain wasn't putting off others who were on the tee and raring to go.

I left them to it and wandered back to the car park. My mobile in my jacket pocket rang just as I reached the car and I was glad it hadn't happened during somebody's back-swing. I remember reading that Tiger Woods's father used to jiggle coins in his pocket and tear velcro as his son was swinging to get him used to distractions, but I didn't think the Moore Park boys would appreciate any distractions.

I answered as I got into the car. 'Hardy.'

'Frank, Cliff. Have you got over your petulance?'

'That what you'd call it? Have you got over your protective instinct?'

'Not doing so well on this, are we? But I've made a few discreet enquiries about … the person in question.'

That was Frank's way of smoothing things down and I knew it. I drew in a breath. Time for reconciliation.

'Thanks, Frank,' I said, in as friendly a tone as I could muster. 'I guess I came over a bit sensitive. The thing is, there's another bloke I'm interested in now.'

'Jesus Christ, you never back off, do you? Okay. Look, I'm in the city. Where're you?'

'At Moore Park golf course.'

His laugh blared in my ear and I moved the phone away.

'You're not! You despise golf.'

'I don't despise it. I'm just agnostic about it. I'm working, Frank.'

'I understand. Why don't I come to your place in, say, half an hour and we'll have a talk. I'll bring lunch.'

'I don't eat lunch, remember?'

'Fuck you, you'll eat lunch and like it. I'll see you.'

After a certain point in life you don't make many new friends, and you have to hold on to the ones you have if you can. Frank and Hilde were precious and their son, Peter, was my anti-godson. With Peter's wife and twins they amounted to something close to family, with my sister in the Northern Territory and Megan flitting all over the place. I hadn't quite realised what a deep hole Lily's death had caused. Mending fences with Frank put me in a much better mood as I drove away.

*

That mood evaporated as soon as I got home. The gate was off its hinges and the front door was ajar. I can be slack about some things, but not about leaving the gate swinging and the house unlocked. Books, magazines and newspapers were strewn all over the living room floor. I went upstairs. Where the computer had been there was a space defined by dust marks. The filing cabinet had been jemmied open and ransacked. Books and other stuff were lying where they had been dropped or thrown. Lily's clothes were in a heap on the floor in the wardrobe. The pockets in the pants and the jacket had been turned inside out.

I remembered that I'd dumped the doctored cigarette packet in the kitchen tidy and I scooted downstairs. It was still there, among the coffee grounds, orange peel and other scraps. The first lucky break in this mess. I had the thumb drive and the disk with me.

There was a tentative knock at the front door. I found my neighbour, Clive, the taxi driver, standing there with a worried look.

'Everything all right, Cliff?'

'No, I've been broken into.'

'Shit, I should've chased after him. Sorry, mate.'

Clive told me that as he'd pulled up a few doors away from his house ten minutes back, he saw someone hurrying down the street carrying something. He didn't think anything of it until he saw that my gate was standing open. The gate is basically busted, and it takes a special touch to keep it on its moorings. I have that touch and I'd demonstrated it to Clive in the past. By the time he'd made the possible connection between the gate and the person carrying something away, the person had driven off. Clive had gone inside and looked for my mobile number but hadn't found it. Then I'd turned up.

'Don't worry about it,' I said. 'I'm insured. Just for the record, what did the guy look like from the back?'

Clive shrugged. 'Big. Dark.'

'Big like tall, or big like fat? Dark like me or dark like Aboriginal or Islander?'

Clive is short, fair and plump. His only exercise is fishing. 'Big like you and dark like you, only bigger, darker and younger. I'd almost say of Middle Eastern appearance, as the expression goes, except ... yeah, no beard. Trouble, Cliff?'

In a way, Clive lives vicariously through me, or did when I was a licensed detective. He was bitterly disappointed when I got scrubbed and now he seemed to be a bit cheered up that there was some action.

'Dunno,' I said. 'Could be. Hope not. What was his car like?'

'Shit. They all look the same these days, don't they? White.'

'Thanks, Clive. I might need a statement from you for the insurance.'

'No problem. What's missing?'

'Computer.'

'Fucker. Hey, he wasn't a junkie or like that. You know—thongs and jeans. He wore a business shirt, pants and shoes.'

I thanked him again and went inside.

Frank arrived a few minutes later. Expecting him, I left the front door open, and he found me in the living room picking up books.

'Untidy bugger, aren't you?'

'I had an uninvited visitor.'

'I thought you had an alarm system.'

'I do. So did Lily. You can get round them if you know how.'

'That's true.' Frank set the plastic bags he was carrying on the stairs. 'Lebanese,' he said, 'and a bottle of that plonk you like.'

'Thanks. Just the job and just for you and this shit I'll break my rule and hoe into the felafel.'

I dropped the book I was holding onto a chair and we went into the kitchen. Frank knew where the corkscrew and the glasses were. He opened the bottle of Houghton white and we spread the food out in its containers on the bench. Plastic forks, paper napkins—nothing flash about me and Frank. I hadn't eaten much in the past few days and found I was hungry. The food was good and the wine was cold.

'So,' Frank said, after we'd lowered the level in the bottle and dug well into the food, 'what was the object of the search, as we say in the courts?'

'Clive next door saw the bloke scuttling off with my computer. The mess suggests he was looking for disks or drives—Lily's. Someone must have nutted out that she worked here a bit.'

'And?'

I pointed to my jacket hanging on the door handle. 'I found it first and carried it on me. I wish he'd come looking for *me*.'

'Mmm, I can imagine. What did you learn?'

'She was working on a few stories, the way she did. Two of 'em look like possibles. Both seem to involve the police, one more than the other.'

'So that's why you want to know about Gregory?'

'And a guy named Kristos.'

I'd never doubted that I could trust Frank. Although our differences regarding professional conduct and temperament surfaced from time to time, we'd been through too much together to ever call it quits. It amounted to him protecting the integrity of the police service, which he still fundamentally believed in, and me trying to stay within the confines of the law as much as I could. Volatile, but viable.

As I slugged down more wine and picked at the remaining food, I laid it all out for him—the removal of DS Williams from the investigation, Lee Townsend's theories about the cleansing of Lily's computer and drives, the apparent laxity of the official investigation. Frank listened in silence.

'That it?' he said as I poured the last of the wine.

'Not quite. Lily's solicitor tells me I've inherited half of her estate. Quite a lot of money. That seems to have sparked a new level of interest in me from this Kristos, whoever he is and whatever rank he holds. It reads like an excuse to me, seeing as how I didn't kill her.'

Frank looked up from loading a fork with tabouli. 'I know that, Cliff. I know that you've only killed two men, both crims and in self-defence.'

'Three,' I said. 'You've forgotten one.'

Frank shrugged. 'Same thing. Two for me. Fucking hated it.'

'Too bad everyone doesn't feel the same. Would this Kristos—'

'Detective Sergeant Mikos Kristos.'

'—be a big, dark bloke who dresses formally?'

Frank nodded.

'There's a fair chance he's the one who nicked my

computer and conducted this bloody search. Mate of
Gregory's, is he?'

Frank's expression spoke volumes of disappointment
and disillusion. Until recently Sydney had been relatively
free of revelations of police corruption. But riots in the
western suburbs and on the southern suburbs beaches had
tested police mettle and divided public opinion about the
usefulness and commitment of the cops. A major scandal
could only do serious damage. Even though Frank was out
of the firing line he still had friends in the force and clung
to a belief in it. I could see his desire to help me struggling
inside him with other impulses.

He made his decision and pushed the food away. 'Vince
Gregory has some glandular disorder that causes him to
smell bad no matter how often he washes or changes his
shirt, but that's not the worst smell about him.'

Frank told me he believed that Gregory was corrupt,
but had high-level protection because he was an effective
player in the complex police/criminal game. He didn't
know the details.

I told him about the two stories Lily had been working
on that seemed to have possibilities of police involvement—the media guy money laundering through a casino,
and the politician protecting some Mr Sin.

'Both big money matters,' Frank said, 'and with the
potential to do serious damage to big reputations. Do you
know the names?'

'No, she used a code in her notes and drafts. I've got some
idea of what it signifies, but it's far from clear. I was going to
sit down with Townsend and try to get a better picture.'

'But?'

'Someone's told me Townsend's not to be trusted.'

'In what respect?'

'I don't know. I'll be asking—it's Tim Arthur, who used to work with Lily. He was playing golf this morning. That's why I was over there.'

'I wouldn't let Townsend know what you know about Lily's writing until you check him out. If that's what got her killed, you have to be absolutely sure that anyone who knows about it is trustworthy.'

I nodded. 'So far, it's just you, me and Arthur. I trust all of us.'

Frank's more of a lateral thinker than me. 'On the other hand,' he said, 'if Townsend's dirty and only recruited you to see if you could bring more of Lily's stuff to light, knowing that you succeeded might flush out whoever killed her.'

'Yeah, me as bait. It might work, but to be honest, Frank, being without standing, as you put it, and with no gun, I'd prefer to come at it some other way if possible.'

Frank smiled. 'You've got another gun, don't tell me you haven't.'

I shrugged. 'You know what I mean. I was lucky to stay out of jail the last time. If I was to wound or kill someone now I'd be gone. Investigation's the name of the game—my journalist mate Harry Tickener should be able to help on Townsend—at least until the approach dead-ends. Then I'd go for the Richo option—whatever it takes.'

Frank said he'd try to make some low-key enquiries about what sort of general connections Gregory had and particularly if there was someone in IT on the inside who was close to him.

'If Townsend wants to get to me before I can check on him, I could tell him that our enquiry's in train and it wouldn't hurt to talk about the break-in. If he's clean he'll be interested, if he's not he'll know anyway.'

We cleared away what was left of the food and put the empty bottle in the box where empty bottles go.

'I'd like to help you clean up, Cliff, but ...'

'I bet,' I said. 'Thanks, Frank. It's a lousy time for me but you're helping. The work helps, too.'

We were on our way to the front door. Frank turned back. 'I need a piss. That wine's run straight through me.'

He knew where to go and when he got back and was zipping up, I said, 'Hey, what about this Kristos?'

'Don't know anything about him.'

'Okay. I was thinking I might contact Williams and try getting something out of him.'

I opened the door and began to usher Frank out. I reminded him of the loose tiles and the dodgy step. A car, slowed by the hump at the top of the street, went past and Frank's body turned rigid as he propped.

'What?' I said.

'Did you see that driver? The one in the light blue Falcon?'

'No. I was worried about you falling down the steps. Why?'

'Fuck it. I haven't seen him for a few years, but I'd swear that was Vince Gregory.'

8

'There's a big apartment complex down the way, maybe he lives there,' I said.

'Last I heard he lived in Longueville.'

'Girlfriend? Boyfriend?'

'Vince Gregory hasn't got any friends of any kind. He was checking up on you.'

'Did he see you, Frank?'

'I don't know. I'll hang around for a bit and see if he comes back.'

We stood on the cracked front path for a few minutes but no one showed.

'You all right to drive, Frank?'

'No. I wasn't expecting to be. I left the car up in Broadway. I reckon I'll be right by the time I walk back there with a coffee or two on the way.'

He set off towards Glebe Point Road and I went inside the house. A knock sounded at the door within minutes. I opened it to see a man in a suit and a light overcoat holding up a card.

'DI Gregory, Mr Hardy. I've been ringing your mobile for an hour or more.'

'It's in the car. I'm still not used to being contactable wherever and whenever. You could've tried the landline.'

'I did. It was out of action. Can I come in? We have to have a talk. Here or somewhere else.'

I let him in and went straight to the telephone. It had been disconnected and it looked as if someone had been investigating the working of the fax and answering machine. They'd have got bugger-all from that.

Gregory looked around the untidy room with an expression impossible to read. I held up the phone jack.

'Disconnected by whoever broke in and did this.'

He nodded. He was in his forties, solidly built but barely medium height, maybe a shade under. Roundish face, closely shaven but with bristles showing already. Thinning dark hair. I moved some books from two chairs and got a bit closer to him. A definite smell, something like old damp socks.

'Have a seat if you want. Sorry not to be more hospitable. I gave a statement to DS Williams. Good man, I thought.'

If Gregory knew I was provoking him he didn't show it. He shrugged out of his coat and folded it over the arm of the chair clear of where he sat. His suit was immaculate. I waited for him to preserve the crease in his trousers the way his type do, but he didn't. He sat back and took a notebook from his pocket.

I pre-empted him. 'What's this in connection with, Inspector?'

'The death of Lillian Truscott. I've learned that you're a beneficiary under the terms of her will.'

'Yeah. That means I killed her. Lock me up.'

'That's not funny.'

'No, it isn't. Get on to something that is.'

'As I passed by, I saw former deputy commissioner Frank Parker here with you.'

'He's an old friend. We had some lunch and shared a bottle of wine. Sorry, it's all gone.'

I was getting to him, bit by bit. He was one of those forceful, middle-sized men of no more than average intelligence, used to having people dance to his tune. You meet them in the police and the army and in politics. Gregory's shirt was done up to the neck and his tie knot was tight. He'd kept his suit jacket buttoned. I was in shirt sleeves and slacks, and with half a bottle of wine in me. Relaxed. He didn't like it.

He shoved the notebook roughly into his pocket, threatening the lining. 'Hardy, I happen to know someone that plays golf at Moore Park. He tells me he saw you deep in conversation with Tim Arthur—who used to make a nuisance of himself with Ms Truscott—looking over a page of notes. And at the wake for Ms Truscott you spent a good deal of time with the poor man's John Pilger, Lee Townsend.'

'Congratulations,' I said. 'You know your subversives and have spies on your books. The Stasi would be proud of you. It's not too late. Get over to the US—spying on their citizens is all the go just now.'

Gregory sucked in a breath to calm himself. As a detective, he'd come up against take-the-piss crims and lawyers often enough not to blow his cool completely. He looked around the room, noting the cobwebs, the missing newel posts on the stair rail, the worn carpet.

'This place is in bad repair, Hardy, and you're out of work. Permanently. Suddenly you're in the money, but you're a chancer, always were. You seem to be conducting an investigation which you're not entitled to do, but it could just be a blind for a crime you committed, or commissioned. What do you think?'

He was a hard man to read—apparently very confident, a quick recoverer from being goaded. If he was involved in Lily's death or covering it up, he was playing an edgy game. He looked rather pleased with his analysis so just maybe he was genuine about it. Confusing.

'I don't think anything about what you just said, Inspector. I didn't let it get anywhere near my brain.'

He got up and collected his neatly folded coat. 'You're by way of being what we call a person of interest. Your alibi has a big time hole in it. I wouldn't be surprised if I found it necessary to pull you in for further questioning.'

I stood as well. You don't let anyone threatening you take the high ground. 'What about this mess? Whoever did it stole my computer. What do you make of that?'

Gregory shrugged into his coat and a wave of the musty smell came towards me. I was tempted to react but didn't. Either he couldn't smell it himself or he wore it as a badge of honour. He was full of energy, full of bounce. 'Like you, I don't think anything, except maybe that you did it yourself. I wouldn't put anything past you, Hardy. What does puzzle me is you and Parker. He was a good cop as far as I know, although you two flew a bit close to the wind recently.'

'You're very well informed. I wonder why you can't find who killed Lily.'

'Give me time, Hardy, give me time. I'll see myself out.'

'No, I'll see you off the premises if you don't mind.'

'Keep your mobile to hand and fix your phone.'

He went out the door and down the path, leaving the gate open. Light rain was falling and he moved smartly to his sky blue Falcon, a model about ten steps in advance of mine, parked across the street. He was a vain man, and thin dark hair doesn't look good wet. I let him have the last word. It didn't cost me anything and if it made him feel he was one up on me that was all right. It was very early in our relationship and I knew I'd see him again.

The smell from Gregory was so strong, a house-proud person would have fumigated. I spent the next hour or so tidying up the spare room and living room and mulling over how things stood. It was confusing to say the least, with Townsend and Frank Parker both pointing the finger at Gregory, while Tim Arthur appeared to have no time for Townsend, the one I'd been thinking of working with.

And, based on our less than friendly meeting, my reaction to Gregory was very ambivalent. If he was up to his ears in some conspiracy to do with Lily's death, then he was a pretty good actor. The removal of Williams and the doubts of Constable Farrow, as reported by Townsend, counted against him. What of DS Kristos? Had he stolen my computer? Was he playing a lone hand or operating with someone who wasn't even in the picture yet?

As Dylan says, 'You gotta *trust* somebody', and I trusted Harry Tickener to give me the drum on Arthur and Townsend. I also needed to get out of the house. Harry, who has done everything in journalism from copy boy in the old hot metal type days to major broadsheet editor, now runs the online newsletter *Searchlight dot.com*—a thorn in the side of the big end of town and anyone else it gets in its sights. Harry particularly likes media scams, so perhaps I could get a line on Lily's story that focused on that. Seemed like a plan.

I drove to Leichhardt where Harry had his office and walked in on him without knocking. He expects me to do that. He has only one part-time staffer, another journalist, and no overheads like a receptionist or secretary. In the nineties there was much talk of the paperless office. It never happened, but Harry got pretty close when he stripped down to the newsletter.

His shiny head was held low over the keyboard, bending his spine the way forty years on the job had carved it, but he can still straighten it, just. A quick glance to identify me and a single finger held up to get me to wait. Harry is a gun-touch typist and I guess, like a pianist, he can take the odd finger away and not lose the beat. He clicked and clacked as I sat down and looked around the big, well-lit space that held books, magazines and framed prints, but none of the stacks of paper you expect to see in writers' workplaces.

'Sorry about Lily, Cliff,' Harry said when he finished. 'You know I don't have anything to do with funerals and wakes.'

I did. Harry's father was a mortician and Harry claims he saw enough death and heard enough talk about it when he was young to last him forever.

'Let me guess,' Harry said. 'Even though you've been wiped as a PEA you're investigating Lily's murder and running into lies, damned lies and bullshit.'

'That's about right. I'm particularly interested in two characters in your field—Tim Arthur and Lee Townsend.'

I put them in that order deliberately and it seemed to have an effect on Harry. 'Oh, shit, those two. No love lost there.'

'How so?'

'They fell out over the rights to a story a few years ago. Some kind of conflict about exclusivity of an interview or some such crap. Right and wrong on both sides, I expect. Townsend got the inside running and got a Walkley.'

'So if Arthur says Townsend's not to be trusted, it'd be over some professional matter rather than meaning he's untrustworthy in general?'

Harry shook his head. 'Aggressive, a go-getter, small man syndrome and all that, but he's a genuine investigative type with a lot of chutzpah.'

'Okay. Have you heard anything about someone in the media being involved in money laundering?'

Harry's desk is bare, no photos to gaze at, no pencil to chew, no paperclips to bend. When he has to think he just thinks. He shook his head. 'Nothing comes to mind now that Kerry's gone, and he was always more into tax minimisation than anything more risky. When you say media person, d'you mean owner, presenter, actor, what?'

'I don't know. Try this on for size—a politician, no gender specified, using influence with the immigration dead-heads to help someone in the sex-slave business.'

'Lily's stories, right?'

I nodded.

'State or federal politician?'

'Dunno.'

'There was a pollie in Victoria allegedly in on an immigration fiddle, but it didn't have the juice that you're talking about. This is young-gun, out-on-the-street stuff, Cliff. I'm just an old man sitting at my desk listening to the winds of change and discord.'

I smiled. 'Purple prose like that and your readers'll be screaming.'

'They scream at me and I scream at them. Instant feedback. It's part of the fun.'

'Thanks, Harry. Townsend has put me on to some things. Looks like I'll be working with him.'

'Good luck.'

Normally, Harry would insist that in return for information he gave me I'd give him the inside track on the story, if there was one. He seemed to sense that with something this personal it wasn't appropriate.

I left the office and walked to the car park behind the theatre complex. I usually park there to put the old heap in the shade and with luck prolong its life. Now, late in the afternoon, it was in deep shadow. As I approached a voice somewhere ahead of me shouted and I looked up in that direction. A strong arm wrapped around my neck and expert fingers felt for the carotid artery. I blacked out, floated, and didn't feel anything when I hit the ground.

9

Getting the blood back to your brain when it's briefly been cut off is very different from the aftermath of being bashed or punched. The first time it happened to me was in the army, when a hand-to-hand-combat instructor did it by accident. A Japanese tough guy did it again somewhat later and not by accident. The recovery has a sense of unreality about it—a feeling of *what the hell happened?*—and then there's a very stiff neck and an awareness of any other injuries incurred. In this case I had a pair of bruised knees and a bump on the forehead where my head had hit the car as I went down, and some aches. Nothing serious, aside from the humiliation.

I hoisted myself up and felt for my wallet in the hip pocket—still there. I reached quickly into the zippered pocket of my jacket. Zip open, disk, thumb drive and page of notes missing. I leaned back against the car and cursed myself for not copying the disk and the notes and putting the thumb drive somewhere safe. My head and jaw ached— another symptom of the brief blackout. For some reason I ground my teeth hard each time this had happened in the past. I was close to grinding them now, in anger.

Unable to break my anti-mobile habit, I'd left the phone in the car. I retrieved it, located Townsend's card in my wallet and called him. You always expect to get a message whoever and whenever you call—nobody's ever actually available, including me. But Townsend was, and he answered.

'It's Hardy,' I said. 'Things are happening and I need to see you. Tell me where and when and make it now if not fucking sooner.'

'You're not making sense, but I'm at home in Lane Cove and you can come here if you want, or I can meet you somewhere.'

Could I drive to Lane Cove feeling the way I did? I thought I could. It's always an advantage to meet someone you're assessing on their home ground, providing no weapons are involved. I got Townsend's address, something a journalist doesn't give out to just anyone, and said I'd be there as soon as I could.

'How soon's that?'

'Why? Got a date?'

'Have it your own way. I'll be here.'

I hadn't meant to antagonise him, but I hadn't meant not to.

Townsend lived in a small sandstone cottage not too far from the Lane Cove National Park. If I sold my terrace I could probably afford one similar—if I wanted to live that far from Jubilee Park, the Toxteth Hotel, Gleebooks, the Broadway cinemas and the Dave Sands memorial. I didn't.

It was dark by the time I got there and he'd thoughtfully left a light on above the front door. I went through a neat garden, up a neat path and some well-maintained steps to a porch with tiles that hadn't lifted and that had been swept clear of leaves. In a quieter mood it would've made me feel ashamed of the look of my place.

I rang the bell. Townsend came quickly to the door, opened the security screen and almost took a backward step.

'What happened to you?'

I hadn't given any thought to my appearance, but when I looked down I saw that my pants were torn at the knees and when I touched the bump on my forehead my hand came away wet.

'Come inside and get cleaned up.'

The immaculate exterior of the house was reproduced inside. Townsend showed me down a short passage of polished boards to a bathroom with all mod cons—spa bath, ceiling radiator, heated towel rails.

'Use what you want,' Townsend said, 'and I'll make you a drink. Scotch, is it?'

'Thanks. A bloody big one.'

I ran water, used a flannel and towel, and dumped them in the basket provided. I've got a milk crate for the purpose, better ventilated. I found bandaids in a drawer and laid one over the graze just below the hairline and above the boxing scars that puckered my eyebrows. I rinsed my hands and mouth and felt considerably better. Out in the passage I heard Townsend talking and went towards the sound.

He was sitting at a pine table in the kitchen with a glass in hand and using his mobile. There was a bottle of Dewar's, another glass, a carafe of water and ice in a bowl on the table.

'Gotta go,' Townsend said and hung up. 'Sorry, Hardy. Have a drink. I wasn't sure of your … proportions.'

I sat and poured a generous measure of the whisky and added ice. I took a long pull and poured some more. I was suddenly very tired and wanted to close my eyes.

'Thanks,' I said after another drink. 'Looks like I landed in the right place.'

'Is anything hurting? You need painkillers?'

I held up my glass. 'This'll do.'

You gotta trust somebody, and anybody who offers you the whole bottle has a good chance of getting the nod. I was in a mood to talk and couldn't see any reason to hold back, so I told Townsend everything from whoa to go. He kept quiet and didn't react, even when I said that Tim Arthur had badmouthed him. I made no excuses about my carelessness in protecting the record of Lily's work, and admitted that I had my doubts about Gregory's involvement. I didn't mention Harry Tickener's reference to the small man syndrome.

I worked my way through the scotch in my glass and eyed the bottle when I finished.

'I've got a spare room,' Townsend said. 'You can stay the night if you're worried about driving over the limit.'

I poured another solid one. 'Thanks. About all I need right now is for the cops to pick me up driving pissed. What d'you make of it all?'

'How much do you remember of Arthur's translation of Lily's codes and initials?'

'Good point. Got a pen and paper? That fucker took my notebook, not that there was anything in it.'

Townsend went into an adjacent room and came out with a pen and a lined pad. I printed out POW, BW, SB and

VER with their equivalents, but not many of the scrambled initials came back to me. I put down IRS, IAD and HON but without any confidence—they could've just been echoes of familiar initials. I tore off the sheet and passed it to Townsend, telling him the initials could all be wrong.

'Not a hell of a lot of help,' he said. 'The upside is that it wouldn't be much help to the opposition either.'

'No. There was enough detail in the stories, as I've outlined them to you, to tell anyone involved what line she was following. He, she, they have the advantage now.'

'She?'

I shrugged. 'Avoiding sexism.'

'Cute. Sorry. This has thrown me a bit. I thought we were on the right lines with Gregory, but you have your doubts. I don't know anything about this Kristos. From what you said, the line on him is a bit ragged.'

'Yeah. Frank didn't know anything about him either, and the identification of him as the one haring away with my computer is very iffy. I've been told he was big and that was a strong arm that went round my neck, but ...'

I shrugged again and the stiff neck hurt. Townsend noticed, left the room and came back with a foil of para-cetamol capsules. 'You're done for the day, Hardy. Have a couple of these and get your head down. We'll look at it all tomorrow.'

I popped a couple of the capsules from the foil. 'How secure's this place?'

'Solid. Alarm system A1 and connected to a private security mob. Why?'

'I must've been followed through the late part of the day. Getting here I didn't notice anything, but my skills are obviously down.'

'I'll give the guys a ring and tell them to keep an eye out.'

'You're not worried on your own account?'

'You kidding? Think I haven't had death threats?'

'That's what Tim Arthur mentioned.'

'Right. Well, you can talk to him about old stories he and Lily covered, but I doubt that's the source of the trouble. Possible, I suppose. Arthur's a prick but he's not dumb.'

I swallowed the capsules with the last dregs of the drink. Townsend showed me where the toilet and the spare room were. After I'd had a piss I went back to the kitchen to see him doodling on the lined pad.

'Last thoughts?'

He looked up, still alert, still energetic. 'Constable Farrow,' he said.

I slept soundly in a comfortable three-quarter bed, woke a bit stiff and sore, showered and used one of Townsend's stack of warmed fluffy towels. He was in the kitchen with coffee brewed and the *Australian*, *Sydney Morning Herald* and *Financial Review* all on the table. I've never known a journalist who wasn't addicted to newsprint.

He barely looked up from one of the papers as I came in. 'Sleep all right? Coffee's made. Croissants in the bag there.'

'Coffee'll do fine.' He was wearing a tracksuit and sneakers. 'Jogging?'

'Walking,' he said, still reading. 'Jogging's bad for the joints. How do you stay trim?'

'Trimmish. Gym, walking, diet, worry.'

'That'll do it. How're the head and the knees?'

'Okay. I might take a couple more of your bombs with the coffee just for insurance.'

I sat and drank coffee, took two more capsules and watched him rapidly process the newspapers while he sipped coffee. He was a picture of concentration; I almost expected him to take notes. Didn't have the nerve to interrupt him. Eventually he pushed the last paper away.

'Sorry. Ingrained habit.'

I nodded. 'Lily was the same. Let's get down to it. Have you got an opinion on which of the two stories is most likely to be the one that got her killed? That's if it wasn't something else altogether.'

'Like what?'

'Dunno. That's one of the things I'll be taking up with your bête noire, Arthur.'

'I'm over that, Hardy. Well over it. Yes, I'd go for the media person laundering money. Dodgy politicians will usually only go so far, at least in this country. They stop short of killing people. In the US and the Philippines, some parts of Europe, there's so much more at stake. I'm going to dig around and see if I can get a whiff of what she was on to.'

'And a possible connection to Gregory.'

'Right. One thing though—can you remember which story VER, meaning a minister of religion, cropped up in?'

I tried. I poured more coffee. After the break-in at the house and the attack on me, the quiet sifting through Lily's work seemed to have happened a long time ago. I tried to recollect my jottings about the codes, their organisation on the page.

'The money laundering story, I think. Can't be positive.'

'Good. It's a hook. And I do so like to see a God-botherer with his nuts in the blender.'

I was starting to like Townsend.

10

Townsend said he'd work on finding out more about the media money launderer, if he could. He had an arrangement to meet Constable Farrow at a wine bar in Chatswood at 6 pm and thought it'd be a good idea if I came along.

'What's her grievance exactly?' I said. 'She's taking a risk talking to you, even if she does fancy you, and an even bigger one talking to me.'

Townsend smiled. 'You underestimating my charisma, Hardy?'

'I reckon charisma's overrated in general.'

'What? Invented by some sawn-off?'

'Your sensitivity's showing.'

He laughed. 'You're a prick, Hardy, but you're right. I don't know what her game is. There's something wrong in that Northern Crimes Unit. It's the line to follow though, you agree?'

'Yeah. But it's all a bit weird—Gregory, Williams, Kristos, Farrow. Who else? What's the big picture? What's the overall structure of the unit?'

'I thought your friend Parker'd fill you in.'

'Not really. Things've changed a bit since his day, as he admits. There's units within units, outsourcing of functions even ...'

Townsend shook his head as I moved to rinse my mug at the sink. 'Cleaner does it all,' he said. 'But you're right again. It's hard to get a handle on anything these days. The word responsibility has dropped out of everyone's vocabulary since this federal government took over. It's all spin, spin, spin, spin.'

On the drive home, I thought over what Townsend had said. It was all true and words were changing their meaning almost daily, as with 'rendition', mutilated by the US military. 'Media' was a loose term anyway. It could mean almost anything to do with communications—satellite services, internet facilitators, software corporations, as well as the good oldies like radio, print, television and film. What this meant was that anyone or any group seriously involved and seriously threatened had a hell of a lot to lose.

I bundled up Lily's clothes and took them to the St Vincent de Paul shop as I'd intended. I threw out two pairs of tights and panties and put her few books on the shelves with mine. Getting rid of the clothes made me feel lousy; keeping the books made me feel just a little bit better. Over the couple of years we'd been semi-together, Lily had given me books as Christmas and birthday presents and written in them. I checked a few of the inscriptions and smiled—Lily's irreverence always made me smile.

Sick of being passive, I hunted out DS Williams's card and called him on his mobile. Got lucky. Got him.

'Williams.'

'Cliff Hardy. I want to talk to you.'

'What about?'

'Come on, Sergeant, you know there's something shitty going on in your unit. It's leaking information for one thing, or it might be disinformation. Doesn't matter. And there's a trail to be followed with a couple of people following it.'

'You?'

'And others. Something's going to blow open sooner or later. Where d'you want to be standing when it happens, and who with? Because I can tell you there's going to be casualties.'

He wasn't dumb. 'If you're so confident, why do you need to talk to me?'

'To speed things up.'

A long pause and I could hear the click of the lighter, the inhale and exhalation. Sometimes a sign of tension, but not always. He must have been out and about somewhere. Where, I wondered? Doing what?

'I suppose we could meet. Where are you?'

Chess, I thought.

'At home. Where're you?'

'Milsons Point. There's a little park down near North Sydney swimming pool. D'you know it?'

'No. Aren't there coffee places along there? What about a pub?'

'Don't piss me off more than you have to, Hardy. I don't want to be seen in a public place with a ... with you.'

I agreed to meet him there in an hour. That gave me time to retrieve the Colt .45 automatic from under the loose floorboards in the hall cupboard, clean and oil it and check on the quality of the ammunition. Frank was right. I had another gun, but only one. The Colt was heavy and I preferred a revolver, but this had come my way a couple of years back without any trace and had been too good an opportunity to pass up. I kept it wrapped in oilcloth in a cool storage place. I'd tested it a few times and found it was in perfect working order. It had been some years since meeting policemen in the open had been a dangerous thing to do in Sydney, but who could forget Roger Rogerson and Warren Lanfranchi?

I drove across the Bridge and down to Milsons Point. I found a parking spot behind the railway station and walked towards the water past the coffee places, lawyers' offices and the Random House building. The day was cloudy and there was a stiff, cold breeze. I was wearing a flannel shirt, sweater and leather jacket and needed every layer. The park was a pocket handkerchief affair with a couple of covered sitting areas. Pretty nice in good weather, bleak today.

The harbour was grey under the cloud, but rain was unlikely at least for a while. There was no one else in the park, so it was far from being a good meeting point if you were worried about being seen.

I sat on a hard seat and began to wonder if I was being set up. The place had some high-rise buildings around it—possible sniper points. I had the .45 in a deep pocket in the jacket. I fingered it and told myself not to be ridiculous. The time for our meeting came and went. I decided to give Williams another ten minutes before phoning. I waited, phoned and got no response—no answer, no message.

I tried to gather my thoughts and impressions about Williams. He'd seemed competent and under control in our first meeting. Maybe a bit pressured and rattled by my phone call, but still coping. Puzzling. I waited a little longer, phoned again and got the same result. I left the park and decided to walk around the area a bit in case he was lurking, keeping an eye on me, wondering what I'd do if he didn't show. The neighbourhood wasn't as parked up as it would have been in better weather. I doubt there were many swimmers, even in the heated pool. A block away, in a cul-de-sac, I saw a red Camry that fitted my memory of Williams's car. There aren't too many of them about in that colour. The street was quiet. I crossed it and approached the vehicle.

DS Colin Williams sat behind the steering wheel, held there by his seatbelt. His head sagged down towards his chest, but he wasn't sleeping. The driver's window glass was starred out around a neat puncture and there was a dark hole in Williams's head—millimetre perfect at his temple.

Williams was a good deal younger than me, had reached a respectable rank in a difficult profession and was, as far as I knew, an honest policeman. Maybe a husband, maybe a father. After Lily's death, I didn't have a lot of space for more sorrow, but there was something about that slumped figure that touched me. A shame, a waste, and someone to blame, possibly the same person who killed Lily. That personalised it and I gave the detective a silent farewell.

Deciding what to do next wasn't easy. I could have just walked away, but there were various means for the police to find out that I'd had an appointment with Williams. An entry in his notebook seemed unlikely, but I'd rung his mobile three times. I decided to play it straight and report it, but there was a problem—my illegal gun. Williams's wound was from a small calibre weapon and there was no chance I could be accused of killing him. But with my record the police were bound to hold and search me and carrying an unlicensed pistol is a serious offence.

I couldn't hide it anywhere near the car because they'd set up a pretty wide perimeter and search it carefully. I moved away from the Camry in case me hanging around there looked suspicious to anyone who happened to be watching. I walked back to the park and deposited the .45 in a rubbish bin after wrapping it in discarded newspaper and folding it into an empty pizza box. I hoped I could get back to it before the bin was emptied. No guarantee.

I went to the covered seat where I'd waited and phoned the police, giving my name, my location and the bare details. I was instructed to remain where I was. A car with two uniforms arrived and I took them to the Camry, standing back to let them take their own look. One of them checked his notepad.

'You say this is Detective Sergeant Williams of the Northern Crimes Unit?'

'Right.'

'And your name is Hardy and you were supposed to meet him here?'

'Hardy, yes. Here, no. In the park where you picked me up.'

'So you found him here and walked back there. Where'd you phone from?'

'Back there.'

The other officer's mobile rang and he had a brief conversation, mostly consisting of grunts at his end. He shut off the phone and took a step towards me.

'You're the private detective who got the flick, right?'

'That's right,' I said. 'No offence, but I'll wait for the Ds before I say anything else. Didn't touch the car, did you, mate?'

I didn't hear exactly what he said, but I thought I caught the word 'arsehole'.

A few minutes later an ambulance pulled up with another police car and then an unmarked. The man who got out of it spoke to the paramedics and briefly to one of the uniformed men. He took a quick look at the body, and then stood twenty metres off issuing directions for the crime scene procedures. A photographer arrived and someone I took to be the pathologist. I was standing well back with a policeman—the one I'd probably offended—beside me and shooting me glances that suggested he'd be delighted if I cut and run.

The detective in the smart suit made several calls on his mobile. He smoked a cigarette and dropped the butt through a stormwater grid. As the photographer and the medical examiner got busy, with the crime scene tape going up and the uniforms keeping away the spectators who'd emerged from nearby houses and buildings, the detective walked towards me. He had dark hair and an olive complexion. He stood about 190 centimetres and would've weighed in at around 100 kilos. He waved the uniform away.

'I'm Detective Sergeant Mikos Kristos, Hardy. Northern Crimes. I can't say I'm glad to meet you.'

A glib reply was on the tip of my tongue but I fought it. Had to be careful.

'I'm sorry about your colleague,' I said.

'Yeah. Good bloke, Col.'

'I thought so, too.'

'Close, were you?'

'I don't think I'll say any more until we're in a controlled situation and I have a lawyer present.'

He pointed to the plaster on my forehead. 'What happened there?'

Was he baiting me? Hard to tell. I didn't answer and watched the paramedics stretcher the body, enclosed in a green bag, to the ambulance. At a guess, the police were telling some of the owners of the cars parked nearby that they'd be free to move them soon. I wondered whether any of the spectators would need counselling. Didn't look like it. Everything was sanitised, clinical.

A TV crew arrived and began filming. Kristos grabbed my arm and hustled me towards a car. I resisted just a little and he almost applied a headlock. I grinned at him and went willingly.

11

The Northern Crimes Unit HQ was in Longueville and it had been a good move to dump the pistol because you couldn't get into the building without undergoing a metal detector check. Kristos escorted me to a room with all the character and personality of an empty stubbie. I said I wouldn't make a statement without having my lawyer present.

Kristos unbuttoned his suit coat and sat in a plastic chair that creaked under his weight. I remained standing.

'Why?' he said. 'You're not a suspect. Even a dickhead like you has the sense not to execute a policeman.'

'Execute. That's an interesting choice of words.'

'What would you call it?'

I shrugged and sat. There are times to stick and times to give a bit. 'I'll meet you halfway,' I said. 'No lawyer and I won't volunteer anything, but I'll answer your questions until I decide not to.'

'Jesus, for a disgraced private eye you come on proud.'

'Family trait.'

He thought about it and eventually shook his head. 'Christ, I'd like to charge you with something and hold you for a while, but I know you'd kick up a stink and have your lawyer up my crack. Anyway, this'll go higher.'

'Gregory,' I said.

He almost laughed. 'I said higher. Right, let's get this over with.'

He switched on the recording equipment and we went through the identification procedure. In response to Kristos's first obvious question, I said I'd arranged to meet Williams to discuss the investigation into the murder of Lillian Truscott.

'Why him?'

'He was the first person I dealt with, after the phone contact from Constable Farrow.'

I watched closely to see whether he reacted to the name. He didn't.

'Why that spot?'

'His choice. He said he was in the area.'

'Did you tell anyone else you were going there?'

'No.'

'Did he mention anyone else?'

'No.'

Kristos consulted his notebook. 'You told the uniformed guys you spotted a car you thought might belong to Williams. How did you know that?'

'He parked it outside my house when I handed over my gun to him a few days ago.'

'You approached, saw him, went back to the park and phoned it in.'

'Right.'

'Why not there and then?'

'I needed time to think about whether to report it or not.'

'Why did you?'

'I'd rung his mobile three times. I thought there'd be a record. I also thought he could have made an entry in his notebook.'

'You fucked up there. Shouldn't tell you this, but you're such a smartarse I can't resist. His mobile and notebook are missing. You could've walked away.'

'So I look better for not doing that.'

'Unless you took them.'

'You don't believe that.' I had to hope he didn't because if he did he'd order a search of the park, including its rubbish bins.

He shook his head. 'No, I don't. But I have to wonder how you're making a living. You've got no job. Mind you, I'm told your house is falling down and I know you've got a crap car, so I suppose you're living on savings. Can't do that for very long. You're bound to turn your hand to something. We'll be keeping an eye on you and come down like a ton of bricks if—'

'That's tonne.'

'What?'

'Move with the times. A tonne of bricks.'

He sat back and looked at me. I never saw a man so keen to hit me except those who actually did. Plenty of them. He was stumped for something to say and in the pause an earlier question he'd asked popped into my mind—the one about telling anyone else where I was to meet Williams. I hadn't, but there was a way someone could have found out—by bugging my home phone. If it had been done it was done cleverly. The jack was out of the wall. You plug it back in and forget about it, don't you? And there was still the suspicion that Kristos had done the break-in. Then there was that instinctive move to apply a headlock. I felt the need to be very cautious.

I said, 'I'm finished talking.'

Kristos stood and buttoned his jacket. His care with his clothing reminded me of Gregory. 'And I've finished listening,' he said. 'You're free to go. We'll need to talk to you again though, Hardy. Could be any time, any place.'

It sounded like a threat, was a threat, but I just nodded. He opened the door and he and a uniformed man standing in the passage escorted me to the front door of the building. Kristos blocked the way, looked out and spun back with a smile on his face.

'I hope those TV arseholes eat you alive.'

They were massed at the bottom of the steps. Must have been other ways out of the building and I could've been given the police coat-over-the-head treatment, but that wasn't the strategy.

I went down the steps and they surged up halfway. Three microphones were stuck in my face and a voice said: 'You found the body, right, Mr Hardy?'

The lifting of my licence had attracted some media attention, so the reporters had no trouble identifying me. My career as a PEA was officially shot, but public recognition would have done it anyway. Despite the posturing of some members of the profession, to be known and highly visible is the last thing a private detective needs. You have to be a chameleon, not a peacock.

'That's right,' I said and pushed on, down at least one step.

'Are you a suspect?'

I laughed and just stood there. They bombarded me with questions which I just ignored. I said nothing at all,

standing stock still. In a way, they're like their viewers—
they have short attention spans. Time is money to their
bosses in a very real sense, and they all know they have to
get their picture and sound grabs quickly and make the
most out of them in strict competition with one another.
Like seagulls, feed them and they stick around, give them
nothing and they go away. I bored them and they left.

I caught a taxi to the coffee place opposite Milsons Point
station, bought a takeaway long black and walked down
to the park. I wasn't followed. I sat and drank the coffee,
dropped the cup in the bin and retrieved the pistol.
I couldn't see the crime scene from down there and didn't
want to. I walked back to the car which had picked up a
parking ticket. With the taxi and the strategic coffee, that
made three expenses, and no client to charge.

I had a couple of hours to kill before the meeting with
Townsend and Farrow in Chatswood. I wondered if she'd
show, after the death of her colleague. I phoned Townsend
and left a message. Thinking about Lily and the break-in
reminded me that Hank Bachelor—a young American,
now Australian resident, PEA I'd occasionally worked
with—had set up business as an alarm installer and anti-
bugging expert. Anti-bugging was something I used to have
the rudiments of, but the advances in technology had
outstripped me. Same with alarms. The system I'd had
installed was out of date. Hank's office was in Crows Nest
and I drove there after phoning him. He was in his
workshop tinkering.

Hank stands around 188 centimetres and would be
about a super-middleweight, maybe a light-heavy. He has

a big man's hands and it was interesting to see him doing delicate work with miniature pieces of equipment.

'Hey, Cliff, my man—' He broke off, remembering about Lily, who he'd met a few times and liked. His tone became more sober. 'How're you doing?'

We shook hands. 'Okay, Hank. No need to tread softly. In fact I'm investigating Lily's death and getting into a lot of shit. It's sort of doing me good.'

He laid the bits and pieces down on his workbench. 'I imagine it would. Want to come inside for coffee or something?'

'No, mate. I won't interrupt you just now. Think you might have a bit of time later?'

'For you, sure.'

I told him about the break-in at my place, the bypassing of the alarm system and my suspicion that the phone was bugged. I gave him a key and asked him to check on how the intruder got in and dealt with the alarm and if the phone had been tapped. He asked a few questions about the alarm and shook his head at my answers.

'Antediluvian, man. Want me to put in something better?'

I wasn't sure I needed it but I agreed. I asked him to ring me on the mobile about the bugging. Hank had given up active PEA work when he married. His wife was Australian, an ambitious professional who wanted to fit in a family somehow, and didn't want a husband running around the city at all hours in low company. I suspected Hank still had yearnings for just that. He confirmed the suspicion.

'Anything else I can do? Need some backup?'

'I'll tell you if I do. You better make yourself known to Clive, my neighbour on the left. After the fuss he'll be keeping an eye out.'

'Will do.' He consulted his watch. 'Be over there in an hour or two. Where will you be?'

'Drinking with a cop and a journalist.'

'Of course. SOP.'

'How's that?'

'Standard operational procedure. I'll get back to you, Cliff.'

Hank is ex-US military and he likes to talk that way when he gets a chance. Luckily, it's not often. I thanked him and we chatted for a few minutes while I displayed a polite, basically ignorant interest in his work. As I drove away I started to think about what I might do as an alternative to PEA work. Nothing came to mind. Depending on the size of Lily's legacy there was no need to think about that for now, or perhaps ever. But there was no way to feel good about it either.

The Falcon chugged on the uphill stretches. Lily had laughed at me for keeping it. I stopped at a light and it was as if she was there in the car with me. She'd scoffed every time I spent money on keeping the car going and shook her head at the glove-box that was still full of cassettes—Piaf, Janis, Dylan, Van Morrison, Dire Straits—long after the cassette player had ceased to function.

'Petrol's going to hit two bucks a litre soon, babe,' she'd said. 'And your fucking V8'll cost you a fortune. You need a fuel efficient compact with a CD player and an air-conditioner that works.'

'It heats in winter,' I said. 'Sort of. And in summer I can park in the shade and wind the windows down.'

But she was right of course. I needed a new car and she'd made it so that I could afford one. The thought made me sad and then angry.

It was getting close to six o'clock and I hadn't had a drink all day. Failing a pub, a wine bar in Chatswood sounded like just the go. Standard operational procedure.

12

Winter seems to come early to Chatswood—maybe a matter of the tall buildings blocking out the light and trapping and channelling the winds. The suburb was a bit of a dump in the early days, with one of the grottiest railway stations you'd ever see. My ex-wife Cyn urged me to locate my business there. She said Chatswood was going to grow. She was right, but I didn't take her advice. They say you can see the Blue Mountains from the upper levels of the towers. Not sure I could've handled that— more of a water man myself. I parked underground, the gloom adding to the winter feel. I didn't know the wine bar and Townsend's directions were sketchy, but a thirsty man can always find a drink. The place was more than half full on a Thursday night and looked as if it might get fuller.

Some wine bars are so dark you trip over the first stool you come to; others are so bright you need shades. The Chat Room, as it was trendily called, was somewhere in between. Non-smoking, soft music, long bar with a section where clustering was encouraged—nice touch—otherwise tables and booths.

I spotted Townsend in a corner booth, obviously chosen for as much privacy as possible. The woman with him had short, no-nonsense blonde hair and wore a white blouse and a dark jacket. I got a glass of red and a complimentary bowl of nuts. I walked over to the booth, wondering which of them to sit next to. Townsend decided the issue by shoving across and leaving an obvious space on his side.

'Cliff Hardy,' he said, 'meet Jane Farrow.'

We exchanged nods as I sat down. She had a glass of white, barely touched; he was halfway through his red. I put the nuts in the middle of the table.

'Saw you on the news,' Townsend said. 'Briefly.'

'That was the idea.'

Jane Farrow picked a few nuts from the bowl, ate them and took a sip of wine. I guessed her age as late twenties. She was good-looking in an unstudied, unadorned way, as if she knew she had no need to tizz up to attract attention from the discerning. Smooth skin, good teeth, firm jaw, wide, full mouth, thick hair framing an oval face. No rings in her ears or on her hands. Strong hands.

I took a pull on my glass. 'You're the fourth person from the Northern Crimes Unit I've met, Ms Farrow,' I said. 'Are you here to tell us what the hell is going on with that mob?'

She glanced at Townsend. 'Is he always this direct, Lee?'

Townsend nodded. 'I'm afraid he is. Of course, he has reason to be.'

I drained my glass and stood. 'Tell you what,' I said. 'I'll go to the bar and get two reds and a white and I'll come back. If you're still talking about me in the third person I'll pour them all over you. Okay? Deal?'

I got the drinks, didn't bother about the nuts, and went back. Jane Farrow had emptied her glass and pushed it to the edge of the table. 'I'm sorry, Mr Hardy. We're all under a lot of strain here.'

I put the glass of white in front of her. 'Strain relief,' I said. 'You're right. Me too.'

I sat and Townsend sipped what was left in his glass before pulling the fresh one towards him. 'You were at the sharp end today, Hardy, trying to contact Williams.'

'No, he was at the sharp end and I think I helped to put him there.'

I told them about my phone-tapping suspicions and the possibility that Kristos was involved. Jane Farrow drank some wine and made a movement that suggested she'd have buried her head in her hands if she lacked the control she obviously had.

'It's getting to be too much for me,' she said.

'What is?' I said.

'D'you know what happens to whistleblowers in the police?'

I could think of a few who'd lost weight and a few who'd lost blood, not to mention their jobs. 'Can't recall any who went onward and upward.'

She almost snarled. 'You're not taking this seriously.'

'Ms Farrow, you haven't given me anything to take one way or another. I don't care about you and I don't care about the police. I care about finding out who killed Lily Truscott and putting that person through as much severe and long-lasting misery as I can.'

'Easy, Hardy,' Townsend said.

'Easy my arse. This is good plonk, but otherwise I feel I'm wasting my time.'

She gave me a hard stare. 'The Northern Crimes Unit is seriously corrupt. Not all of the divisions, not everybody, and not all the time, but there're people pulling strings, making sure that things run the way they want and taking drastic steps when certain matters come up.'

'Matters like?'

'Like murder. Lillian Truscott wasn't the first journalist to be killed. Do you remember the Rex Robinson case?'

I didn't, must have been too caught up in my own problems, but Townsend obviously did. 'Freelance,' he said. 'Killed in his car about a year ago. Brakes failed and he went through a railing into the water. Where was that again?'

'Northbridge. I'm sure he must've got on to some of the stuff I'm talking about and was … taken care of.'

'By a policeman?' I asked.

She shrugged. 'Or someone contracted by a policeman and police used to take the investigation precisely nowhere.'

'That's a throwback to the old days—the green light and all that stuff.'

Jane nodded. 'Bit before my time, but if you say so. You need to understand the history of the unit.'

Townsend sat very still. I looked at him and he looked steadily back. 'This is more than I've heard from Jane so far,' he said.

'Let's not start talking about someone present as if they're not here again,' I said. 'You've got my attention, Ms Farrow.'

'Jane, for Christ's sake. I'm putting my life in your fucking hands, both of you. Let's pretend we at least know each other.'

Townsend put his arm around her shoulders and she let it stay there. She was very stressed and had done a good job of concealing it, but the facade was cracking.

A man like me, with a battered dial and the hooded, distrustful eyes inherited from my Irish gypsy grandmother, has difficulty looking comforting. I've been told I have a voice like Bob Hawke on a good day, so I can't soothe that way either.

'I'll say this,' I said. 'I think you're a very brave woman and I admire bravery. My guess is you want our help— Lee's and mine—as much as we want yours. Can we start from there?'

Jane drew in a deep breath and drank some of her wine. Townsend did much the same and they exchanged smiles.

'You fucking charmer, you,' Townsend said.

I put on the brogue. 'Irish.'

'Hardy's not Irish,' Jane said.

'And other things. Can we get a feed here? I'm bloody starving.'

We went next door to a fish restaurant. Suited me. Townsend had grilled sardines and salad and ate like a bird, while Jane Farrow and I ploughed into the barramundi. She seemed to appreciate the extra time it gave her and I wondered if she might change her mind. We shared a bottle of white.

I felt I should get the ball rolling as we cleaned up the chips. 'Aren't you worried some of your colleagues might see you in this company, Jane?'

'No. The high-ups have their designated watering hole, the Lord of the Isles in St Leonards, and the drones have theirs, or they go home to their wives, girlfriends and boyfriends.'

I nodded. 'Lee, what's on your mind?'

'You know me,' Townsend said. 'I'll stick a camera in anyone's face, put a foot in any doorjamb. But this is different. I'm genuinely worried about what might happen to Jane if … if she puts flesh on the bones of what she's just told us.'

'I'm doing it,' Jane said. 'I can't stand it any longer. Let whatever happens happen.'

She told us that the Northern Crimes Unit had been put together from a group of other police outfits and was designed to liaise closely with business, community, political, educational and church organisations to provide a coordinated anti-crime set-up that would be a model for other areas.

'It was kept hush-hush, but it sounded good and quite a lot of people in the force, good people, were attracted to join it. But it turned out to be bullshit. None of the organisations could get on together. The business people were out for a big buck like always, the God squaddies were getting madder and more right-wing by the minute, the state and private schools were at each other's throats. The whole thing fell apart. The good people left and the force had to offer accelerated promotion and special conditions to attract people. That's why I joined—to get on. But a lot of the others who joined saw the opportunities to run profitable sidelines—mainly escort agencies, immigration scams, and supplying drugs to the affluent middle-class workaholics.'

'How long has this been going on?' I asked.

'At its worst, a couple of years.'

Townsend said, 'How was it kept under wraps?'

'It's the lower north shore and the harbour beaches, Lee,' Jane said. 'Nothing nasty is supposed to happen here, and a lot of bribery money gets spread around to keep mouths shut.'

We ordered coffee and I had to wonder if Townsend had a tape recorder on him somewhere. It was hard to imagine him letting all this just go out in the ether. As for me, I wished I could have taken notes, because some of the things Jane said chimed with what little I'd gleaned from Lily's files—immigration fraud, the sex industry. The stuff about drugs to the well-heeled was new, but maybe Lily'd had a code for drugs that I didn't know.

'You look sceptical,' Jane said to me.

'No, not really. It's just so big and … amorphous.'

'Lily must have got wind of it somehow,' Townsend said. 'She never hinted …?'

I shook my head. 'Never, but she was like that. She didn't talk about her stories until they were nailed down.'

Townsend said, 'The questions, as far as Cliff's concerned, correct me if I'm wrong, are—who did she get the information from and who found out about it?'

'Right,' I said. 'And what are the questions for you, Lee?'

'How to write, broadcast, film, whatever, the story and get it out while protecting Jane.'

The coffee arrived.

I looked at Jane, who was spilling packets of sugar into her cup, stirring, adding more, stirring, until Townsend gently stopped her.

'Jane?' he said.

She stopped stirring, took a sip of the coffee and grimaced at the sweetness. 'I grew up in Mt Druitt,' she said. 'We weren't exactly welfare dependents, but not far from it. I got into the University of Western Sydney and did okay. I was pretty good at everything. Not brilliant, but okay. My mum drummed into me that what you needed was a secure job where you could get on. A police recruitment guy, and a woman, came out to the uni. I applied and got accepted, went to the Academy. There were no fucking HECS fees then at the Academy the way there are now and I knew it'd be a while before I earned enough to have to pay back the uni HECS. I sailed through, did a stint in the country and was told about the openings at the Northern Command.'

She picked up her coffee cup, but I pushed mine across to her and put one packet of sugar in it and stirred. She smiled her thanks, had a drink, and went on.

'Do you two city types understand that I'd never really been to Sydney at all? You can't imagine what growing up in the west is like. You know the water's that way and the mountains are over there, but they don't seem to have anything to do with you. I'd had a few fleeting visits as a kid—school outing stuff, the Olympics, something forget-table at the Opera House one night. I'd never properly seen the harbour, let alone the northern suburbs and beaches. I was knocked out when I saw how terrific the place was, after where I'd come from. The whole scene got to me, the beauty of it, and I was happy working here. Then I saw what was going on in the unit. I knew that they were—fuck, how to put it?—polluters, with their scams and deals and cover-ups. I just want this beautiful place to be made beautiful again.'

13

A while ago Lily and I had been to an exhibition of police photographs dating back to the early years of the last century and running through to just after the Second World War. The show was at the Police and Justice Museum—sepia and black and white stuff, very stark, very dramatic. The notes that would have put the photos in context had mostly been lost, so the images had to speak for themselves with a minimum of interpretation. They did. They showed the underbelly of a city founded by law-breakers and their punishers which bore their stamp down the generations. I loved Sydney, but I never imagined it could be as beautiful on the inside as the outside. Not a single street of it. After working on the seamy side for as long as I had, and associating with police and others who did the same, I knew that corruption and violence were an inescapable part of the scenery.

'You've got that sceptical look again,' Townsend said.

'No. I'm just trying to remember when I last thought a beautiful place was capable of being good as well.'

'You think I'm naive,' Jane said.

'Maybe, but in a bloody nice way.'

'I'm not naive. What I just said might sound that way, but I've seen people corrupted and destroyed.'

I nodded. 'These people, these string-pullers, do you know who they are?'

She hesitated before replying. 'Yes. I've got a list.'

'In general terms?'

'A big developer, two politicians—one local, one state—an owner and an operator of several clubs.'

'No minister of religion?'

'No, why?'

'Doesn't matter. What area does this unit cover?'

'Not that much—North Sydney, St Leonards, Crows Nest, across to Greenwich, and to Mosman on the east and up to Balmoral.'

'Lot of people there.'

'All the more to exploit.'

'All the more to get upset.'

'Look, I'll tell you how it works. Give you an example. A developer wants to take over a site, put up a block of apartments, but it's zoned commercial. He funnels some money to the councillors and they get a zoning variation so the citizens don't have to be consulted—commercial-cum-residential. Up go the flats, but the developer has a criminal record and shouldn't be in business. That's when my colleagues step in. They let him get on with his building on the understanding that a certain number of the units are set aside for the girls and that brings in the drugs, automatically. The same police talk to the girls' suppliers and make arrangements for other people living in the flats, or nearby, to be serviced. The cops take a percentage. It's all kept quiet. Everybody's happy.'

Townsend looked worried. 'Wouldn't it change the character of an area? Wouldn't someone notice and complain?'

Jane shook her head. 'People are too busy to notice. Do you know what sort of hours they work to keep their jobs and meet their mortgages? But you're right, some have complained. They're either intimidated or bought off. For a few, like Rex Robinson and Lillian Truscott, the intimidation went all the way, as I said. Anyhow, that was just an example. The development scams, rezonings, kickbacks to councillors—no one cares anymore. Just like no one expects the politicians to accept that the buck stops with them. It does, but not the way whoever said it meant.'

'Harry Truman,' Townsend said.

I said, 'The man who dropped the atom bombs.'

Jane shrugged. 'There you go. The other thing is, it's intermittent and spread out and happening on a large and small scale all over the place. Especially at the beaches. A fuss blows up over something, usually some conflict of interest within the organisation, as I like to think of it. It's not like it's a criminal syndicate. It's a loose organisation with people operating on a nod and a wink and a brown paper bag—the way it was in Queensland under Joh Bjelke-Petersen, I've been told. They settle it down and things go on as before, after a pause.'

'What you say's very convincing, Jane,' I said, 'but can you supply the evidence?'

She fiddled with the coffee cup. 'This is the hard part. I've kept a detailed record of things I know happened— names, place names and dates. And I have personal knowledge of amounts of money involved in ... some of the minor matters. I've got all this in a safe place, at least I hope it is. But I'm not going to come out of this squeaky clean. I've taken kickbacks myself. I had to, or I would've been sidelined. Or they would've made it so hard for me I'd have had to quit. That's probably going to be difficult for you to understand.'

Townsend said, 'Not necessarily, but it's a complication in terms of your credibility.'

'I know, but I've got every dollar documented and it's all put away with the other stuff.'

She was very pale and her hands were shaking. Townsend put three fingers on her forearm and leaned a bit closer towards her. He was good at the body language—comforting, not condescending. I was sympathetic, but I didn't feel I was getting a whole lot closer to my focus—who, in this tangle, spoke to Lily and who found that out and took the next step. Jane said it wasn't her who put Lily on the track, but could I believe her? Professional, highly competent, concerned woman. Who more likely?

'Cliff?' Townsend said. 'Where've you gone?'

'I'm sorry. I'd like to know what your next move is, Jane. I mean, you've accumulated this … data. Why act now? And how?'

In fact, I had more questions: *What was your relationship with Gregory and Williams? How did you team up with Townsend? Why were you happy to have me along at this meeting? Why are you prepared to blow the whistle now?* But I let the questions I'd put stand.

Jane stopped fiddling and shaking. She drank some water, drew in a deep breath, and colour returned to her face. She glanced at Townsend and then looked straight at me. 'I met Lee. As far as I could tell he wasn't trying for a story, he was just …'

'Attracted,' Townsend said. 'Right.'

'So we talked, and then Lily Truscott was killed. I knew the name and that she was a journalist, and as soon as Colin Williams was reassigned, I made a connection to the sort of stuff I've been talking about and I spoke to Lee a bit more … specifically. And now we're here.'

'Lee,' I said, 'sounds as if most of this is all news to you.'

'It is,' Townsend said. 'Jane has been very guarded. She gave me a few more hints when she heard I'd made contact with you.'

'Why's that?' I said.

'Because I want protection,' Jane said. She broke off and took in another deep breath. 'You're driving, Lee. Can I get a brandy?'

Townsend ordered two—one for her, one for me. Not my favourite drink by a long way, but I wanted to give her some kind of support and Townsend was bound to get the best stuff. I'd do my nocturnal sobering walk trick if necessary. The drinks came and Jane took a slug. Me too. Smooth.

'I've got a plan,' she said.

Jane Farrow's plan was for her to meet with Vince Gregory, who was unhappy about her having broken off their affair. She intended to confirm that it was all off between them, to insult him and then tell him she was planning to report the corruption within the Northern Crimes Unit to the police ombudsman.

'He'll go nuts,' she said. 'He'll be furious with me on both counts, but he's a cold, calculating bastard and he'll try to persuade me not to talk. I'll say I need certain guarantees from Gary Perkins, he's the Chief Super, and pretty much at the heart of the corruption, or very close to it.'

'They'll kill you,' Townsend said.

She nodded. 'They'll try, but we set the meeting up so you can film and tape the discussion and the deal we strike, and we rely on Mr Hardy here to protect me. We film the attempt on me as well. A bit before it gets too heavy, I hope.'

'It's madness,' Townsend said. 'Far too dangerous.'

Then I got an insight into the obsession that had hold of her. She became almost coquettish: 'Don't you want the story, Lee?'

Townsend said nothing and she turned her attention to me. 'If we get Gregory and Perkins on toast, they'll dob in the others. They'll talk. They'll deal. It's your best chance at getting a line on who killed Lillian. They'll know.'

'You'd give me a free run at them?'

'Yes.'

'Off-camera?'

She shrugged. 'Why not?'

Obsessed, ruthless. Trustworthy? Impossible to be sure.

'Jane,' I said, 'I can see what's in it for Lee and possibly for me, but what have you got to gain? Just supposing it goes according to your plan, and I wouldn't bet on it, you'll be finished in the police force. A lot of mud'll stick to you. Your future'd be pretty bleak. You might write a book, might sell the film rights, but ...'

'It stinks,' Jane said. 'People are getting hurt. It sickens me. Call me a martyr.'

The use of that word worried me a lot. In my book, martyrs of all kinds are deluded—paradise doesn't exist and neither does a clean city. To do him credit, Townsend, who had most to gain, was as uncertain as me.

'It's not something to rush into,' he said. 'There might be other ways.'

'There aren't,' she said.

'When were you thinking of making your move?'

'I can't stand it much longer. As soon as possible—a week?'

Townsend shook his head. 'It'd take that long at least to set up the locale and other necessary arrangements.'

Jane finished her brandy. 'Ten days, max!'

'Or?' I said.

'Or I find someone else to do it with.'

That's where we left it. Townsend paid for the dinner and took Jane off, whether to her place or his I didn't know or care. I watched them walk away, holding hands. She was ten centimetres taller in her flatties, but Townsend held himself so well and moved so fluently the difference wasn't as noticeable as it might have been.

I decided that I was sober enough to drive, but I went for a long walk anyway. I had a lot of thinking to do and walking helps. The rain held off, but those Chatswood canyon winds got to me and made me step up my pace. Lily and I used to walk around the streets at night, in Glebe and Greenwich, burning off the evening meal calories, processing the booze, talking. We talked about politics, books, films, people. We told stories from our past that helped to bind us together. When someone knows that much about you and you know a lot about them, there's a connection. It helps you to avoid mistakes, anticipate needs, keep things flowing. I missed those walks.

I found myself thinking more about Lily than Townsend and Jane Farrow and her extraordinary claims and proposal. I got lost, and had to concentrate to find my way back to the car park, so I stopped thinking about the evening's developments altogether. I retrieved the car, paid the fee and drove out into heavy rain. More thoughts of Lily, who'd always mocked my clunky wipers.

I drove carefully in the sort of moderate to heavy traffic that seems to be on the move in most parts of Sydney day and night. For a couple of kilometres I found myself behind one of those drivers who hit the brakes unexpectedly and too often, and change lanes without signalling. I surprised myself by remaining patient. I turned the radio on but I could scarcely hear it over the drumming of the rain. I was back in my own territory before my mind could focus on the shape of things again. One thought came through clearly: *Find out a lot more about Jane Farrow.*

part two

14

Townsend rang me the next morning. Hank Bachelor had left a note saying that he'd found the bugging device and removed it. He'd also installed an up-to-the-minute alarm system geared to a private security mob he recommended.

'We have to talk,' Townsend said.

'I'll say we do. I've had this phone debugged, so we can talk on this line.'

'I'm on my mobile. Should be okay.'

Thank God he didn't call it *my cell.* 'Is she with you now?'

'No. She's back on the job, bright and early. Have you ever had a relationship with someone you knew was obsessed, maybe unstable, but you wanted her just the same?'

I thought of Glen Withers, Marisha Karatsky. 'Yeah, once or twice,' I said.

'What happened?'

'Fun at the time. Didn't work out well for either party long-term.'

'What d'you think about Jane?'

'I'm not sure whether you're talking about you and her, or her and this scheme she has.'

I could hear his sigh down the line. 'Neither am I.'

'I'd like to get her on a polygraph to ask if she was the one who talked to Lily.'

'No chance of that. She'd drop us like hot scones. I'm not wide-eyed, Hardy. I know she's using me.'

'Us.'

'Right, but at one point you told her she was convincing.'

'Good recall, Lee. One of the things I wanted to ask— did you have a tape running?'

He laughed. 'Jesus, I was tempted, but no I didn't. And just as well. She patted me down, which I didn't mind, and insisted I leave my briefcase in the car.'

'D'you have any idea where this safe place she spoke of might be?'

'Not a clue. I get your drift. It'd help if we could get a look at the material she claims to have.'

'How was she this morning? How did you read her?'

'She was very edgy. Dreading going to work, but going just the same. A prime candidate for 'stress leave. I care about her, and I'm bloody conflicted.'

We talked it over for a bit longer and took some comfort from having ten days before Jane put her head in the lion's mouth. I suggested to Townsend that he tap his sources for confirmation of some of the details of what Jane had told us about corruption north of the Bridge.

'I could do that. What'll you be doing?'

'Investigating Gregory, Kristos and this Perkins character. Seeing where they live, what they drive, who they fuck.'

'How will you do that? Through Frank Parker?'

'And in other ways. One thing I should tell you. Apparently I've come into property and money through Lily's will. Kristos said that made me a suspect.'

'Fuck, why are you telling me that?'

'Just so you'll know how complicated it all is.'

What I didn't tell him was that the person I was intending to investigate was Jane Farrow. Duplicitous, but what was he keeping back from me? Bound to be something.

A good hacker can get into most computer files and Phil Lawton was one of the best. A long way from being a nerd, he works out at the Redgum gym, runs half-marathons and the City to Surf, and can talk intelligently on quite a few subjects. About the only similarity between Phil and the stereotype of the computer geek is that he has a beard— well, more of a stubble. I went to the gym hoping I might catch him there, but I was told he'd been and gone. My knees were still sore and I didn't feel like a workout, so I headed for the spa and soaked and thought. Then it was coffee at the Bar Napoli, an often repeated routine, except that my mobile wouldn't ring with Lily telling me she was heading to Brisbane. Or that she was back from Canberra, and how about dinner?

Phil works at whatever computer experts do, from home in Annandale, where he converted a garage into a temple to Microsoft, Google and the digital solar system— make that the universe. No point ringing him, he never answered.

I drove to his house via a couple of sneaky streets, a route that'd let me know whether I was being followed. No tail. Phil's street dead-ends at a set of steps leading down to

Booth Street. I parked near the foot of the steps and walked up. Exercise wherever and whenever you can. I pressed the buzzer and didn't need to speak. I knew Phil could see me in full colour from several angles. The house is nothing to look at, but the security is Fort Knox-like. A soft hum sounded and I was able to open the security door. A chime, and I could open the main door after that.

Once inside, I knew where to go and that I'd be tracked. The workroom door opened when I was two strides away and Phil had swivelled round in his chair to greet me as I stepped into the softly murmuring, light-blinking sanctum.

'Hi, Cliff,' Phil said. 'Can you hang on a minute while I zap this fucker?'

I found a non-electronic place to sit while he spun around and tapped keys. He spun back.

'So, healing cut and bruise on forehead. Slight stiffness of movement. Same old Cliff. Sorry to touch a nerve, but aren't you out of business?'

He didn't know Lily and I didn't want to go into the details. 'I'm sort of freelancing,' I said. 'Consulting, you might say.'

'Good for you. So, whatcha want? If it's in my power ...'

Phil was in my debt. One time when he was pushing iron without a spotter, the upright he slotted the weight into gave way. I was there and managed to grab the weight and hold it until he scrambled out from under it. Otherwise, he'd have had a bar with 70 kilos attached coming down somewhere near his chest or head. Almighty crash when I let it go.

I told him I wanted information on a person who'd attended the University of Western Sydney and the Goulburn Police Academy and was a current member of the state police service.

He whistled. 'Don't want much, do you? The university's a snap, but the police stuff. Shit, they've got all sorts of firewalls and cut-outs.'

'Can it be done?'

He waved his hand at the banks of screens and printers and scanners and God knows what else. 'That's the beauty of it,' he said. 'Everything that's out there is in here. It's Aladdin's cave, mate, and all you need is about a thousand and one ways to say "Open Sesame".'

'Right,' I said.

He moved his chair along to another machine. Over his shoulder he said, 'Name?'

I told him.

'DOB?'

'1980, approximately.'

'Shit, that's all? Okay, leave it with me.'

I'm no computer expert, but I've paid my fees and have access to the databanks of a few of the broadsheet newspapers. The computer in my office in Newtown is a laptop, even more of a clunker than the desktop one at home, but it can do the job if you're patient. With cyber stuff, I am—let's say still a bit amazed at what the bloody machines can do. I hadn't been to the office in weeks, had given my notice to quit, and would have to clear it out very soon. It had been an okay place to work, hard to get a park though, and on this Friday afternoon I had to circle several blocks to get anywhere reasonably close.

Evidently whoever had broken in and stolen the computer from Glebe hadn't known about the Newtown office or had reasoned that Lily wouldn't have worked there. They were right; no self-respecting journalist would have used the old Mac with its antiquated operating system and floppy disks.

The office was grotty at the best of times, but when I was working there regularly I'd occasionally go over it with a broom, duster and a wet cloth. After the recent neglect, the cobwebs had gathered and the room and its small alcove smelled musty. A hundred years of dust sits in the building and filters down. There was a layer over every surface, and a few big cockroaches scuttled for cover from the shelf where I kept the coffee and sugar.

I opened the windows to let the petrol fumes compete with the mustiness and gave the chair, the printer, the mouse pad and space for a notebook a few wipes. I turned the computer on and let it plod slowly through its paces. The coffee was stale but I brewed it up anyway. While I waited for what I wanted to come up, I thought about the few years I'd worked here and some of the people who'd sat across from me with their troubles, their lies, their threats. Some of them I missed, others I wished I'd never laid eyes on.

I trawled through the papers looking for articles by and about the late Rex Robinson. He was an old hand, a freelancer who'd broken a lot of stories back in the seventies and eighties but seemed to have tapered off through the nineties and after. The occasional piece still turned up—crime reporting—but the material was thin and there was plenty of harking back to earlier days when he'd given evidence to enquiries of one sort or another into the police service. One thing was relevant: his later stories, bland though they were, focused on the area covered by the Northern Crimes Unit.

His last published piece had a little more muscle than the others and dealt with the death of an Asian prostitute in North Sydney. The very young woman, who'd overstayed her visitor's visa, had been released from a detention centre, apparently by mistake. The official verdict was suicide by drug overdose, but Robinson had implied there was more to it. One sentence read: 'A former police officer from the Northern Crimes Unit said that the coroner's verdict was "unsafe".'

Townsend's recall on Robinson's death was accurate. His fairly aged Volvo had gone through a railing and into Sailors Bay at Northbridge. Police divers recovered the vehicle and the body the next day when the broken rail was noticed. The inquest was held soon after and no significant evidence was offered other than the police opinion that the vehicle was in such poor repair that mechanical failure was the likely cause of the accident.

All this had happened when I was in the throes of my trouble with the Police Licensing Board and I was scarcely glancing at the papers. If there'd been anything on television I hadn't seen it. Now, scanning the follow-up news coverage and somewhat perfunctory obituaries, I gathered, reading between the lines, that Robinson was an unpopular figure. He was an arrogant big-noter who others judged to have achieved, briefly, an eminence far above his merit. Tributes from the journalistic profession were dutiful rather than sincere. I didn't recall Lily ever having mentioned him.

I printed out some of the material and highlighted bits of the printout, especially the stuff about the sex-worker released from detention and the 'former police officer from the Northern Crimes Unit'. It had been a sad insight into what seemed like a sad life. No Walkleys, no books, no television spots. Robinson had two failed marriages, a bankruptcy and two DUI convictions. But at least it was some confirmation of what Jane Farrow had told us.

15

Talking to key-tappers and tapping keys is all very well, but it doesn't feel like real work. I didn't want to just sit around waiting for people to get back to me with information that might or might not be useful. I felt I owed it to Lily to *do* something.

I drove home, still cautious about a tail, made a stop at an ATM to draw out some cash, and investigated my closet. I had a blazer, worn but respectable. I had dark trousers and a burgundy shirt, both recently dry-cleaned. I had a matching pair of black socks and slip-on Italian shoes that only needed a touch of the Nugget brush to get rid of the white mould. After a shower, a shampoo and a shave, I reckoned I was ready for a Friday night out at the Lord of the Isles hotel in St Leonards where, according to Jane Farrow, the Northern Crimes Unit brass gathered.

In the past, the bars favoured by the cops around Darlinghurst and the Cross were bloodhouses. The television series *Blue Murder* got it about right, with a little exaggeration for dramatic effect. There were drunken brawls between the cops, between the crims and between the cops and the crims. The occasional gunshot, the odd thrust with a broken glass. I was there myself once in a while, keeping my head down, but I saw an eye gouged out and half an ear bitten off. Blood everywhere.

I doubted that a modern North Shore police hangout would be in any way similar and I was right. The Lord of the Isles was a fancied-up old pub that was working the Scottish theme to death—tartan everywhere, claymores on the walls, full kilted figures in glass cases, bagpipes. A sign outside advertised a Tuesday trivia night with a well-known stand-up comic as moderator, a mid-week happy hour and Friday night exotic dancing in the Robert the Bruce bar. Hoots! Whoop-de-doo.

It was a bit after nine when I got there and the place was in full swing. The main bar was crowded with the younger set drinking European beers and Jim Beam and cola. The Royal Stuart bar was smaller, quieter, with older people, both sexes more formally dressed—the men, and some of the women, in suits. A few small groups stood at the bar, but most of the drinkers were at tables with bowls of pretzels and nuts, and short drinks.

I went to the bar, ordered a scotch, and saw Vince Gregory and Mikos Kristos at a table with two other men. Nothing advertised them as cops. They could've been advertising executives, merchant bankers ... A few other tables were occupied by similar groups of men. Possibly more police.

Gregory saw me first. He spoke to Kristos, who turned around to look at me. The other two didn't react. Kristos made an elaborate show of finishing his drink and came over to the bar for a refill. He got it and moved along to stand near me, out of earshot of the other drinkers.

'What the fuck are you doing here, Hardy?'

'It's a free country, last I heard. And they take my money here just as they take yours. While money's being mentioned, what'll you have?'

'Fuck off.'

'What about a wrestle? Graeco-Roman? Remember Roy and HG? That was brilliant.'

He stared at me as if I'd lost my mind, turned on his heel, started to walk away, but Gregory joined him. The musty smell about him was less strong, though still there. Maybe he'd showered and changed his shirt before coming to the pub. He'd had a few drinks and his tie was askew; his thin hair was sticking up at the back. His five o'clock shadow was a ten o'clock stubble. I thought of Lee Townsend's immaculate grooming and how Jane Farrow appeared to appreciate it. I couldn't see how she'd be attracted to Gregory. Unless there was a reason that had nothing to do with grooming.

Kristos shook his head and urged Gregory back to their table. I left the bar but I hung around. Gregory and Kristos left the pub soon after, looking worried. The other two went to the Robert the Bruce room to join in the fun. I followed them, bought a drink and took a seat. It was essentially a strip show, again with the Scottish theme—kilts and sporrans, dirks and tam-o'shanters coming off to AC/DC and Rod Stewart. Very tasteful. The room was darkish away from the stage, and I kept out of the eyeline of the two men anyway. One checked his watch and nodded. Soon after they were joined by two stylishly dressed young women. Escorts. A bottle of champagne arrived and their evening got underway.

I'd rattled Gregory and Kristos a bit, I thought, but hadn't achieved much else. I was about to call it quits when a woman walked into the room, looked around and spotted the group I was watching. She was in her thirties, tall, casually dressed, neither particularly attractive nor plain. She strode through the tables, reached the one where my party was sitting and shouted something I couldn't hear over the music. One of the men got to his feet and she picked up a champagne glass and threw the contents in his face. She grabbed another glass and emptied it over one of the women.

The man who'd been attacked was sitting now and wiping his face. The other one was dealing with the escort who had champagne ruining her hairdo. By then I was at the table and had the woman by the arm. She was swearing and unsteady, whether from shock or insobriety I couldn't tell. I got a firm, incapacitating hold on her, and moved her away before anyone at the table could react.

'Security,' I said as loudly as I could. 'I'll deal with this.' I half carried the struggling woman out of the room. She fought me, but she wasn't in a fit state to do much damage and I managed to get her into a quiet corner away from the noisy bars.

'Don't struggle,' I said in her ear. 'I'm not security and I'm not a cop. I want to help. Let's get out of here.'

She was at the end of her tether, went limp and let me lead her out of the hotel onto the pavement, where a cold wind swept down on us. She wore only a light blouse and I took off my blazer and draped it over her shoulders as I propelled her along the street.

'Help?' she said. 'How can you help? He's dead. They bloody murdered him, the bastards.'

She wore a wedding ring. 'Mrs Williams?' I said, still with a grip on her arm.

'Yes. Who're you? I don't know you.'

'I met your husband,' I said. 'I thought he was a good man. I need to talk to you.'

I found a coffee bar not far away and got Mrs Williams seated. She was still agitated, but calmer, resigned to being moved about. I decided she wasn't drunk. I ordered two flat whites. We sat quietly. She handed me my jacket with what was almost a smile.

'Thanks,' she said. 'I really freaked them, didn't I?'

'You did a good job of that all right.'

The coffees came and I encouraged her to put sugar in hers. She did and drank it scalding hot without seeming to notice. She had a strong, pale face, dark hair and the look of someone usually well in control. Not now. She played with the spoon, moved her free hand up to her face and looked for a moment as if she was about to bite her fingernails, which were short and well-shaped. She saw what she was doing and pulled her hand away.

'Haven't bitten my nails since I was a kid,' she said. 'Wouldn't have a cigarette on you?'

'No, sorry.'

'Good. I'll be right back on them if I'm not careful. Gave them up when I got pregnant with Lucy. Col tried but he couldn't. I made him smoke outside.'

Tears came to her eyes and she wiped them away with a napkin before drinking more coffee.

'Okay,' she said. 'I suppose I should thank you. Those bastards could've given me a rough time. They're mates with everyone in that place. You seem to know who I am. Who're you?'

I told her as much as I thought she needed to know to understand why I'd butted in. She listened quietly, told me her name was Pam when I told her mine. She stopped fidgeting and nodded when I finished.

'Col told me about the journalist being killed.'

'Did he tell you he'd been taken off the case?'

'Yes, but not why. He never talked about his work in detail. Bottled it all up. But when he got shot I knew who'd done it.'

I sensed she didn't mean it literally and I waited for her to elaborate.

'That was Gary Perkins back there, a Chief Superintendent and a bloody crook. I don't know the other one—some sleaze or other. They're hand-in-glove with the money men.'

'They? You mean Perkins, and who else?'

She shook her head. 'I'm not sure. I shouldn't even have known that much, but I heard Col on the phone a few times when he didn't know I was around. He was getting more and more upset as time went on. I tried to persuade him to transfer, even resign, but he wouldn't. Once he said, without meaning to, that he couldn't.'

'How did you interpret that, Pam?'

'I didn't like to think about it, but I reckon he must have been caught up in some of the corruption. Turned a blind eye, took some money, I don't know. The other day I talked to a friend of mine who was the wife of another man in the unit. He died of cancer. She said he told her before he died that Perkins and some of the others were thieves and murderers. She said her bloke was scared for his life because Perkins didn't trust him and took him off a case that was a murder Perkins was covering up. When I heard that I put two and two together with Col being taken off the case involving your ... partner. And I just snapped. I'm on this lousy medication for depression. It screws me up. But I took some and had a big vodka to give myself courage, and you saw what I did.'

'You've put yourself at risk.'

'I don't care. My sister's staying with me for a bit. She lives in Queensland and I'm going to move up there with Lucy. Get away from all this shit.'

'I hope that's going to happen soon.'

She smiled and some of the tension went out of her face, leaving it alert and appealing. 'Tomorrow. I'm not really brave. I just had to do *something*.'

'I understand. That's why I'm trying to get evidence on why Lily was killed. I'm picking up bits and pieces and you've helped me.'

She shrugged. 'Can't see how. I haven't got any evidence.'

'Do you think your friend might have?'

'Hannah? I don't know. She might. She's still furious about Danny's death. She reckons the strain of working in the unit brought on the cancer. Probably not true, but ...'

'I'd like to talk to her.'

'You're serious, aren't you?'

'Very.'

She looked hard at me and seemed to be making a judgement. 'I'd say you're every bit as tough as them. I'd love to see them screwed. I'll phone Hannah tomorrow before I go. If she's willing to talk to you, I'll phone you and tell you where to find her and that.'

I gave her my card. She said she'd driven from Lane Cove and was all right to drive home. I said I'd follow her to make sure she was safe. Her car was parked around the corner from mine and I gave her my jacket again for the short walk.

The wind was cold and she drew the jacket around her. She put a hand into one of the pockets and took out my keys.

'What d'you drive?'

'An old Falcon.'

'An honest man's car.'

She put the keys away and took out my Swiss army knife. 'Col always carried one of these.'

'Do you know anyone in the unit you can trust?' I asked.

'No. I've had condolence calls from some of them and I expect I'll get cards, but it'll be bullshit.'

'A woman called me to tell me about Lily. A detective named Farrow. Is she—?'

'Jane Farrow? She threw herself at Col at a party. That slut. She'd fuck anything that moved. She's the last person I'd trust.'

16

What had started out as a fishing expedition had possibly landed a fair-sized catch. Pam Williams struck me as a sensible, level-headed woman who'd allowed herself one uncontrolled outburst. Fair enough. If Hannah whoever-she-was, widow of Danny whoever-he-was, had any hard evidence to use against Perkins and the others, perhaps Jane Farrow's dangerous plan wouldn't be needed.

After following Pam to a modest block of flats in Lane Cove—a fair distance and a few grades down from Townsend's bijou cottage—I drove home in a better frame of mind. It was late and I hadn't eaten. I felt like a solid drink and thought I'd better act on the Graham Greene principle—I'd read that Greene's only real interest in food was to act as a blotter for alcohol. Scrambled eggs and toast go down as well at midnight as at any other time, I reckon, and particularly with a solid scotch and soda.

I got the notebook I was using to replace the stolen one and started to make my diagrams and doodles. I've done this for years—writing names, connecting them with arrows and dotted lines according to the firmness of the information, and scattering exclamation points and question marks through the scribble. Tim Arthur had told me not to trust Townsend, but Harry Tickener had provided a satisfactory explanation for that. But here was a whole new expression of distrust—Pam Williams vis-a-vis Jane Farrow. Given that I'd already wondered why Farrow would have had any intimate connection with Gregory, her name now deserved a heavy underlining and a big question mark.

Townsend rang in the morning to ask about my progress. I claimed to be making some without giving details. I said that the name Gary Perkins, mentioned by Jane Farrow, had come up and I was looking into him.

Townsend didn't sound very impressed and I suspected he knew I wasn't telling it all. Perhaps I should have added a few notes of frustration. I tried to cover up by asking him about his progress, but he saw through that.

'You're hedging, Cliff. I thought we were in this together.'

I had to come clean, not only to stay onside with him, but to test his commitment to the investigation, given his relationship with Farrow. 'I'm hearing things about Jane,' I said.

'So?'

'You've had time to think about it. What's your take on this plan of hers?'

'I don't like it, but she's got us over a barrel. Unless we come up with something better she'll go ahead anyway. There are other journalists, other private eyes for that matter. And you aren't even one of them, strictly speaking. So, have you come up with anything better?'

'Maybe.'

'I've got a call waiting. Get back to me when you decide what the fuck you want to do.'

He hung up and I couldn't blame him. He could tell I felt myself to be on shifting ground and that doesn't inspire confidence. I moped around the house for a while and then the phone rang.

'Hardy.'

'Mr Hardy, this is Pam Williams. I'm calling from Mascot. Lucy and my sister and I are on our way to the sunshine state.'

'Good for you.'

'Hannah Morello is gung-ho to talk to you. Here's her phone number and address.'

She rattled them off, with the airport lounge noise in the background. I scribbled them down and thanked her.

'Maybe you can come back when all this is over,' I said.

'I don't think so. Know what? Sydney's overpriced and overrated. Bye.'

Good exit line. I rang Townsend and told him I had an informant ready to talk about police corruption in the Northern Crimes Unit—possibly in possession of hard evidence.

'You were going to keep this from me?'

'I just got confirmation. I'm inviting you to sit in on the meeting, on one condition.'

'Which is?'

'That you don't tell Jane anything about it until we follow it up, check it out, see what we can make of it.'

A hesitation, then he said, 'Agreed.'

'How will I be sure? We're talking several deaths here.'

'You have my word.'

I'd rather have had his mobile phone and every other means of communication he possessed under my control, but there was no way. Still, I played it cautiously. I said I'd call him back with a meeting place and time.

I rang Hannah Morello and told her who I was.

'I've been waiting for your call,' she said. 'I want to talk to you.'

'I've got your address. When?'

'Just as soon as you can get here.'

Promising. She lived in Drummoyne. I said one hour. I rang Townsend and arranged to meet him at a point some distance from the Morello address in forty minutes. I drove to Drummoyne, scoped out the Morello house, and took up a spot where I could see Townsend arriving. I'd made sure I wasn't followed; I wanted to be sure he wasn't. Dead on time, he arrived in a sporty yellow Mazda. The place I'd chosen had a view of the water at Iron Cove if you walked fifty metres. Townsend sat in his car for a few minutes, got out and went to where he could see the view. Who wouldn't? The day was clear and the water was blue and Sydney's waterways have an attraction all their own, no matter what Pam Williams thought.

A few cars passed, none slowed or circled. Looked to be all clear. I drove along and pulled up beside Townsend. I got out. He turned, saw me, turned back.

'Great view,' I said. 'Used to be more interesting when there were working docks and shipyards. That's what I think. What d'you think?'

He didn't take the bait. 'Trusting, aren't you?'

'No. One of the reasons I'm still alive.'

'What was the point?'

'To make sure you weren't followed.'

'That is, I didn't tell Jane.'

'Among other possibilities.'

'You're a bastard, Hardy.'

'Wish I had a dollar … Let's go and talk to a woman who might be able to help us a lot.'

Hannah Morello lived in a terrace house in a street a block or two back from the river. Maybe a glimpse of the water from the top storey. Not many cars parked in the street at that time of day. We opened the gate and in two strides—two and a half for Townsend—were at the front door. I knocked and the door was opened almost immediately. Hannah Morello was lean and dark with a beaky nose and a strong chin. She wore jeans and a sweater, sneakers.

'Mrs Morello, I'm Cliff Hardy. This is Lee Townsend. I know I didn't say he was coming but—'

'I know Mr Townsend from the television,' she said. 'Please come in.'

She ushered us into the front room. It was a sitting room with a TV and stereo set-up, pleasantly furnished. A wall had been knocked out to make a double space out of the two front rooms with the second one serving as a dining room. Standard terrace renovation—a big hammer, an r.s.j. and a skip, and you're in business.

We sat on vinyl lounge chairs around a low table. She offered us coffee. We refused. She sat very straight in her chair, tense, but with a determined look, while I ran through a quick preamble on what we were doing, what we expected to do and how we hoped she could help us.

'I can,' she said. 'I've been waiting for the chance. Didn't know what to do, but when Pam Williams phoned me I knew my bloody chance had come.'

Townsend shot me an enquiring look. I hadn't told him about Pam Williams, but it was the quickest of glances so as not to distract her.

'We know that Gary Perkins and others are corrupt,' I said. 'We know that they've connived at murder, maybe committed it or had it done. But we haven't yet got any proof.'

'I have.'

Townsend leaned forward and his handsome face took on an expression of confidence and reassurance. This was the way he appeared on television—uncannily bigger, stronger, smarter.

'When you say that, Mrs Morello, what do you mean?'

'I have photographs my husband took.'

'Photographs that incriminate Perkins?'

'And that Greek.'

'Kristos,' I said. 'What about Vince Gregory?'

She shrugged. 'Dunno about him.'

Townsend took a device the size of a cigarette packet from his jacket pocket. 'This is a miniature digital recorder,' he said. 'Would you be willing to let me record you when you put the photos on the table here and tell us briefly what they are and how you come to have them? You don't have to act, just speak clearly. I can keep your face out of the frame or have it pixelated if you wish.'

She didn't even blink. 'No problem,' she said. 'And bugger that. I'll look the lens full in the face if you want.'

Townsend nodded. 'Let's do it.'

She left the room and I heard her mounting the stairs. Townsend smiled at me. 'Technology, Hardy. Out of your depth, are you?'

I'd read about these gadgets, never used one, but I knew the language. 'Hope you've got a big enough memory card.'

He smiled and checked the thing over. 'I never did hear about this Pam Williams, although I can work out who she is.'

'You've heard now. She put me on to Mrs Morello just before she decamped lock, stock and barrel to Queensland. It worries me the danger this woman is putting herself in.'

'That's why I offered to mask her identity.'

'Big of you, but that won't do it.'

'Let's see what she's got first. Play it by ear after that. She looks pretty ... capable.'

Hannah Morello came back carrying a manilla folder. She stood in the archway looking at Townsend, who lifted his camera and nodded. She walked into the room and spilled the contents of the folder onto the table. A couple of photos fell off the edge. Nice drama. Night shots. Black and white, at least a dozen of them.

Townsend filmed the action and then lifted the camera to film her as she sat down. She'd tidied her dark mane of hair and put on a little makeup. Changed her sweater for a dark silk shirt. She used her left hand to point to the photographs, her wedding ring glinting.

'My name is Hannah Morello,' she said. 'I am the widow of Detective Sergeant Daniel Morello of the Northern Crimes Unit of the New South Wales Police Service. These photographs were taken by my husband. They show Detective Senior Sergeant Mikos Kristos murdering the journalist Rex Robinson. My husband died of cancer some time after he took these pictures. I found them later among his effects. I believe the stress he underwent as a result of what he discovered about his colleagues caused or accelerated his cancer. I want justice.'

17

Hannah Morello gestured for Townsend to turn the recorder off.

'From things he said, my guess is that Danny had talked to Robinson about what was happening in the unit. Perhaps it was off the record. I'm still guessing, but I think he didn't trust Robinson. You'd lose the ability to trust, working in that place. Somehow, he was on the scene when this happened. Maybe he was following Robinson, or even Perkins. I don't know.'

Townsend and I examined the photos. They were blow-ups and a bit grainy but clear enough. The sequence was: a man—bulky in a heavy coat and unidentifiable with a cap pulled down low—leaning in to talk to a driver with another car behind; Kristos leaving the second car; a man, presumably Robinson, being threatened with a pistol by the one who'd been talking to him; Robinson getting out of his car; Kristos putting Robinson in a headlock; Kristos and the other arranging a limp Robinson behind the steering wheel of his car; the man leaning in across the body, presumably turning on the engine; Kristos behind the wheel of the second car with his front bumper only inches from the back bumper of Robinson's car; a blurry image of a moving car; a shot of a broken railing from a point overlooking a steep drop to a body of water.

'Well?' Hannah Morello said.

Townsend carefully, almost reverently, arranged the photos into a neat pile. 'Extraordinary,' he said. 'Can I record again with you saying how you came to find these and why you haven't done anything about them until now?'

'Why not?'

I put up a warning hand. 'Just hold on a minute. Do you realise the danger you're putting yourself in, Mrs Morello? When Kristos knows about this material he'll probably try to kill you.'

It was clear she hadn't considered it. 'Why?' she said. 'There's the evidence against them, cut and dried.'

'No, he's right,' Townsend said. 'Photographs can be faked or doctored with modern technology. This set needs your statement to make them solidly credible. Have you got children?'

That hit home. 'Two,' she said, 'Josh and Milly, six and eight years old.'

'You'd need protection,' I said. 'Someone to stay here to keep watch on the children, and on you when you're out and about.'

She lost some of the upbeat manner. 'I hadn't thought it through. How long would we be talking about?'

I said, 'Difficult to know. There'd be an enquiry and a trial. You'd be in danger all that time.'

'Are you trying to discourage me, Mr Hardy?'

'No. I just want you to know what you're up against.'

'There could be another way,' Townsend said. 'Is this the only set of photographs?'

'No, Danny was a keen amateur photographer. He had a darkroom and all the gear. He developed two sets. What do you mean, another way?'

My question exactly.

Townsend tapped the photographs. 'These incriminate Kristos, but we know he's in close association with at least a few other police in the unit, some of them with higher rank. If pressure could be brought to bear on those people, they'd give Kristos up in a flash. If his mates desert him and he's charged, denied bail, he's virtually impotent. You'd be that much safer.'

'So some of the bastards would get off the hook?'

'Not entirely—dismissal, lesser charges, that sort of thing. It'd still break up the organisation effectively.'

She gave us both a long, steady look and made her decision. 'Would you arrange the protection you're talking about while this dealing was going on?'

Townsend said, 'We will. Cliff can carry some of the load and I'm sure he has contacts. What do you say, Cliff?'

Townsend was hard to read. One minute he was hot for the story and fuck-you-jack, the next he was all compassion and conciliation. I thought I knew what he was up to, but this wasn't the time to debate it. For as long as knowledge of the photos stayed strictly with the three people in the room, Hannah Morello was safe. The second the word got out, her life's possibilities sharply diminished.

I decided to stall. 'Your husband never said anything about having the photos?'

She shook her head. 'Never. He might have meant to, but his cancer was incredibly aggressive. He went from being able to talk and to see the kids to needing heavy sedation in a matter of days. After that he ... he really wasn't there.'

'How have you managed financially?'

'Danny was in the force for nearly twenty years. His superannuation was good. I inherited some money about twelve years ago and we bought this house when the prices were much lower. It was a bit of a wreck but Danny fixed it up. Not much mortgage and I work part-time as an architect. He was a good man, Danny. He only joined the Northern Crimes Unit because it had promotion possibilities. I wish he hadn't.'

'What's your point, Cliff?' Townsend said with just a touch of impatience in his voice.

'I'm not sure. I think Mrs Morello should have someone to advise her.'

Townsend was good. He showed no reaction, merely looked at the woman. She reached over and picked up the photographs, flicked through them, put them down.

'Danny wasn't the bravest man in the world,' she said. 'He should have taken these straight to the Internal Affairs people or the police ombudsman, yelled blue murder and let the world know what was happening. I would have backed him because I could see what working there was doing to him. I could've taken the kids off somewhere. But he didn't. I hate to think he was somehow compromised. I don't believe that. I think he just didn't have the nerve.'

This was a strong woman, a fact-facer, potentially an excellent witness. I found her now looking straight at me.

'Pam and I talked for a while last night, Mr Hardy. She told me what you'd done for her, what you said about your partner being killed and about Col. To put it bluntly—she was impressed by the way you behaved. I agreed to talk to you and the last thing she said to me was, "I'm sure you can trust him", meaning you. Pam's smart and I reckon she was right. You say I need someone to advise me. Okay, I'll be advised by you.'

Townsend and I didn't speak as we walked back to our cars. I had the folder of photographs in my hand. Townsend had his film. I'd told Hannah Morello to sit tight for a day while we arranged for her safety and the use of her evidence. We reached the cars and stood awkwardly, at odds, looking at each other. He was immaculate, I wasn't. He was driving a forty thousand dollar car, I wasn't.

'You were playing a strange game in there,' he said.

'So were you.'

He looked at his watch. 'Tell you what, let's go and have lunch and talk about it.'

'I don't eat lunch.'

He laughed. 'You can push a salad around, have some juice. We really need to get our lines straight here.'

His composure irked me, but I knew my response had been petulant. I agreed to meet him in a Balmain restaurant I vaguely knew. I tapped the folder and pointed to his briefcase.

'Nobody hears about this until we have our talk, right?'

'Yes.' He reached into his pocket, took out his mobile phone and handed it to me. 'You can follow me and see that I don't stop to use a phone. What more can I do?'

I followed him into Balmain, busy on a Saturday, and after trying a few side streets with no luck we finally found places to park. I returned the phone and we walked back to Darling Street and along to a small cafe-cum-restaurant in an arcade. Townsend ordered fish for himself, a Greek salad for me and a small carafe of white wine with two bottles of mineral water. When the wine came he poured half-glasses and topped them up with the water. We drank, no toasting.

'What's your main concern?' he asked. 'I know it involves the Morello woman's safety.'

I still couldn't decide how far to trust him, where his loyalties lay, what he was prepared to risk. On the drive another thought had forced its way forward in my mind. Getting Kristos convicted and dismantling the corrupt component of the Northern Crimes Unit were all very well, but I needed leverage to find out who'd killed Lily or ordered it, and I wasn't sure how to get that.

I told Townsend about that thought as he ate his fish and I dealt with my salad.

'More to it than that,' he said. 'You're not exactly a poker face, Cliff. You don't trust me. Why's that?'

Time to come clean. 'It's not that I don't trust you. I'm worried about your association with Jane Farrow. I'd be more inclined to say that I don't trust her.'

He dropped his fork, the only clumsy action I'd ever seen from him. 'Jesus Christ, think of the risks she's taking.'

'Why's she taking them? Why not walk away?'

'A matter of principle.'

'Struck a lot of that in your profession, have you, Lee?'

He picked up his fork and prodded at the remains of his meal, but he'd lost his appetite. I decided to follow up the possible advantage. 'Have you ever been up close to Vince Gregory?'

'No, why?'

'He smells. Some kind of glandular disorder, apparently. I can't understand why a clean-cut type like Farrow would be attracted. And there's another thing. This won't please you.'

'What?'

'Pam Williams—now I know I didn't tell you about meeting her and what happened last night and all that. It doesn't matter now. She confronted Perkins and one of his mates while I was keeping an eye on them, and she gave them shit. She struck me as very much like her friend, Hannah—smart, tough, honest. She told me Jane Farrow had come on strong to her husband. I'm sorry, Lee, but there's something about Farrow that troubles me.'

Townsend's control was slipping. 'Are you saying you met her? She came on to you?'

'No, nothing like that.'

'Fuck it, I thought … I don't know what to think. What's in your bloody brain?'

'Just that I know what you're thinking. A double whammy. The Morello evidence *and* whatever Jane can get them to admit. Right?'

'I don't like it, but the Morello evidence isn't enough. It could just leave Kristos holding the bag, despite what I said to her back there. You know how enquiries and prosecutions can work. The deals they can cut.'

'Yeah. If I knew Kristos had killed Lily, I'd just go up against him with the photos, make him tell me why, pretend to deal, and dump him in the shit.'

'You would, I'm sure. But it isn't his style. You know that. It's more likely to be the guy with the gun in the Morello photos—well in with the cops. Probably the same one who killed Williams, and we have no idea who that is. We need leverage to get someone like Perkins or Gregory to tell us.'

I filled my glass with wine and didn't dilute it. Townsend and I had kept our voices down because there were others sitting nearby. A few glanced at him, but none came up for his autograph. A waitress took our plates and we both ordered coffee. I had a new and uncomfortable feeling, the result of having been with two people who'd lost their partners, with me in the same boat. My empathy was all with them, tinged with anger.

'I don't want you to tell Jane Farrow about the Morello photographs until I've checked her out more thoroughly.'

'You're checking on her?'

'In depth.'

'Shit. I was thinking of suggesting that I *did* tell her, and that we mount the protection on Mrs Morello, so if any attempt was made on her, we'd know that Jane was …'

My smile stopped him. 'You were willing to dice with a woman's life to find out if your lover was on the straight. And you call me a bastard.'

'I was only thinking about it. Being pragmatic.'

'The last refuge of a scoundrel.'

'Wasn't that patriotism?'

'Applies, though.'

The coffees came. Gave us more time to think. Stir, taste, stir again.

'We're both holding evidence,' I said. 'I've got the photos, you've got the film. Neither has much bite without the other.'

'True.'

'Two days, nothing said to Jane Farrow. Agreed?'

'Okay. I wish I could think of something to hold you to, but you're too slippery.'

'You can pay the bill while you're thinking.'

He produced a fat wallet, took out a credit card and waved it, the gesture stopping just short of arrogance. The waitress brought the bill, took the card, returned the folder and Townsend signed, leaving a tip.

'Thanks,' I said.

He nodded, still irritated.

'Hey, you're Mr Pragmatism. You might even pretend to go a bit cool on her to test her reaction.'

'Fuck you,' he said.

18

As it was on my way and I was impatient, I called in on Phil Lawton to see what his web trawling had turned up.

'Impatient bugger, aren't you?' was his greeting.

'Yup.'

'Still working out?'

'When I get time.'

'Use it or lose it.'

'Phil …'

'Just playing you along, mate. Yeah, I've checked out Jane Margaret Farrow, DOB 27/1/79. Scored in the high nineties in the HSC. She graduated in Arts at the University of Western Sydney in 2001, second class honours, division one, majoring in sociology and economics. Honours thesis on the 1979 Woodward Royal Commission into drugs. Represented Australia at the 2000 Commonwealth Games in pistol shooting, finishing fourth. Close, but no cigar. Am I going too fast for you to get this down?'

One of Phil's typical jokes. I wasn't taking notes—he was drawing attention to his total recall of the information, one of his many talents. I didn't bother to reply, and he went on.

'Goulburn Police Academy 2001. Fitness level top ten percentile; rated excellent all categories; probationary constable, Mt Druitt 2001–02; posted to various Sydney stations 2002; promoted to detective 2004, appointed to Northern Crimes Unit 2005.'

'Thanks, Phil. That it?'

'No. There's a gap in there I couldn't probe. These sorts of records are date sensitive. They're coded, but that's not usually a problem if you—'

I held up my hand. 'I don't need to know.'

'Okay, she disappears between late 2004 and early 2005. I tried to trace her in other ways—illness, overseas travel, phone, electoral roll, credit cards and what-have-you, with no result. She sort of vanishes during that period, say for six months.'

'Jesus, are we all documented that closely?'

'Not all, some—probably be most before too long the way things are going. Have to be protected against terrorists, ha ha. Know any, do you? I'm sure I could organise a bounty for dobbing them in.'

'Great. Now that you've looked at this stuff, how would you rate her progress as a police officer?'

'Are you kidding? Fucking rapid. Mind you, when she was in uniform she made some good arrests and had stellar showings in court that stamped her as promising. No getting away from that. Plus, the service was looking to promote women and the Northern Crimes Unit was in the rapid promotion loop it seems. Natural place for her to go.'

'That's right.'

'The gap's the thing that takes the eye. Nature hates a vacuum; me too. I'll keep at it. Can't bear to be snookered.

There's another possibility. I hate to admit it but there could be a pathway I haven't cracked.'

I thanked Phil and asked him if there'd be any trace in the records of his search.

'You're joking,' he said.

'Just playing you along. I'll spot you at the gym next time you try to lift more than you should.'

He gave me the bird and turned back to his god.

There was a scattering of phone messages and emails when I got home. Nothing important. Viv Garner wanting to know how I was doing. Tim Arthur saying he'd looked through his files and memory and couldn't locate anything he and Lily had worked on in the past that would be likely to have brought about her death. Frank Parker checking in with nothing new to report but concerned that I might go feral—that sort of thing. Bills in the letterbox along with junk mail. Bin the one, curse the other.

I was restless and decided to go for a long walk. I needed the exercise after so much sitting. The knees felt better and I reckoned keeping the bits and pieces moving was the go, rather than letting them calcify and lock up. Medically specious probably, but it had worked for me over a long time and many injuries. The clear day had persisted although a breeze had started with a bit of snow-fields in it. Tracksuit time. I'd left the .45, rewrapped but not hidden, in the locked cupboard under the stairs, which happened to be where I'd hung my daggy tracksuit last time I'd used it. I saw the bundle and had thoughts: *Were Kristos's break-in and headlock—if they had been his—just warnings? If so, what about now, after I'd spooked him and*

Gregory at the pub? Were Perkins and any others involved in the deaths of Robinson and Williams aware of me and threatened? What game was mystery woman Jane Margaret Farrow really playing?

I wasn't going to skulk and hide, but it made sense to take precautions. I stripped down, put on the tracksuit and sneakers, and slid the .45 into a bumbag.

I walked up Glebe Point Road to Broadway, around Victoria Park, back through the university and down John Street to the Crescent to wind up with a circuit of Jubilee Park. Five kilometres, maybe six—parks, higher learning, traditional houses, renovations, new apartment blocks, water views. The walk brought me out at the bottom of my street. It has nooks and crannies—lanes leading to adjacent streets, a couple of sets of steps and a postage stamp park. I did a few ups and downs on the steps, stretching the hammies. I looked over from the top step and stopped dead.

A light blue Falcon was parked in a lane with its nose a few metres back from the footpath. It was half hidden by plane trees and positioned to give it a perfect view of my front gate. From whichever direction I approached, I'd be in the crosshairs.

The steps I was on led to a narrow lane between two of the larger sandstone houses in the street. Million dollar jobs. Over the years, the owners had several times applied to have the pathway closed and its right-of-way status revoked. A few of us, on doubtful heritage grounds, had enjoyed ourselves resisting the applications and so far we'd been successful. I went back along the path, pushing aside the overgrown honeysuckle the two owners had planted to inhibit access.

I circled around the next street and came up the lane behind the Falcon, staying in shadow, silent in my sneakers, and with the .45 in my hand. The person in the driver's seat of the sky blue Falcon was solidly built, with thin, dark hair, scalp showing, besuited. Detective Inspector Vincent Gregory beyond a doubt.

I stayed a few metres back from the car, well-hidden but puzzled by his apparent inattention. He was almost slumped in his seat, but he had the window down. Did he have a sighted-in, silenced sniper rifle at the ready? No way to tell. It'd take a rifle to do the job from this distance. How long would it take him to bring it into play on me if I jumped him at the open window? Too long. But what if he had a pistol in his lap, or in his hand?

I decided that was ridiculous. I turned away to muffle the sound as I cocked the automatic.

What are you doing? I thought at that moment. *Putting an unlicensed gun on a serving senior police officer?* I had a moment of indecision at that point. Frank Parker's message on the answering machine came back to me: *Don't go feral on this, Cliff. You'll only come to grief.*

I hesitated. *How much more grief could I come to? Lover gone, career finished.*

Gregory stayed slumped in his seat. *Light a cigarette,* I pleaded. *Use your hands.* But he didn't.

I went forward as quickly and quietly as I could and had the muzzle of the .45 in his right earhole before he could move a muscle. There were no weapons in view. He had one hand on the steering wheel, the other flat on the seat beside him.

'Don't even twitch,' I said.

The musty stench from his body was stronger than ever. As he drew in a breath and let it out slowly, I caught a strong smell of alcohol.

'I won't,' he said. 'I don't believe you'd shoot me, but I'll still do what you say.'

'What makes you think I won't shoot you?'

'Because you want to know who killed Lillian Truscott and why, and I can tell you.'

'Why would you do that?'

He reached up and pushed the pistol away. 'To save my skin, Hardy. To save my fucking skin.'

19

I didn't like him, I didn't trust him and I didn't take any chances with him. I made him get out of the car, open his jacket and turn around to be sure he wasn't carrying a gun. If any Australian policeman, private eye or crim has ever carried a pistol in an ankle holster, I've never seen it. With my gun in the pocket of my tracksuit pants I propelled him ahead of me, across the street, through the gate and up to the door. I had to reach for my keys and if he had any intention of attacking me this was his moment. He stayed as passive as a lamb and he hadn't said a word on the way.

We went inside and I kicked the door shut. He turned around slowly.

'You don't need the gun,' he said.

Now that I was face to face with him the change since I'd last seen him, only a matter of hours back, was remarkable. The flesh on his face seemed to have sagged, fallen in, giving him a haggard look. His suit could have done with a brush and his top shirt button was undone and the tie knot was sloppy.

He reached into the side pocket of his jacket and took out a half-full flask of Johnnie Walker. The Gregory I'd first met would never have ruined the sit of his suit with something like that.

'Wouldn't mind a drop of water,' he said.

I pointed down the passage towards the kitchen and followed him through. His previous arrogant strut had been replaced by a shamble. He slumped into a chair. I ran water into a glass and handed it to him. He topped it up with the whisky, drank half, held on to the flask.

'You could arrest me for possession of an unlicensed pistol,' I said, 'and for threatening a police officer. Deprivation of liberty, maybe. Why don't you?'

He sniffed as though he had a cold. 'I'm not arresting anybody. Not anymore. What I'm concerned about is not getting arrested myself.'

He poured some more whisky, put the flask in his pocket and made a half-successful attempt to pull himself together by straightening up in his chair and patting down the hair that had stuck in patches over his skull. He nursed the drink.

'You know what's been going on in the unit, don't you, Hardy?'

'I've got a fair idea. The top cops are in with the money men and a couple of pollies doing all sorts of fiddles. Bribery and corruption. One murder has been covered up; another is in the process of being covered up. Then there's the murder of Lily Truscott—that's not going to be covered up as long as I have breath in my body. The thing is, Gregory, how do you know that I know this stuff?'

His eyes were red and he had difficulty focusing. 'I know you talked to Pam Williams. Perkins didn't know who you were when you butted in at the pub—thought you were the bouncer, like you said—but I did from his description of you.'

I shook my head. 'I talked to her, but all she had were suspicions. You're spooked and I'm glad to see it. You're right. I *know* things, but the question remains—how do you know I know?'

'You've been talking to someone in the unit.'

'Maybe.'

'Kristos.'

I did my best not to show surprise. 'Maybe.'

'Has to be. Didn't fool me when you provoked him for the cameras where Williams got killed. Same when he fronted up to you at the Lord of the Isles. That was a blind. He's in it with you and I can guess where he's going to lay the blame.'

The man was delusional and paranoid, carrying a burden of guilt and fear of retribution. I had to guide him carefully in the right direction.

'Do you know who killed Rex Robinson?'

'I know Kristos was there.'

'So do I.'

'He told you? I bet I know who he said did the killing. Me.'

I shrugged.

'I didn't. I wasn't there. He's cutting a deal, isn't he? He gets out from under while Perkins and the rest of us go down.'

'It could work out like that.'

'No, it won't. Kristos had Robinson and Williams and your girlfriend killed.'

'*Had* them killed,' I said. 'Who by?'

He shook his head. 'Not here, not now, not just to you. I want your mate Townsend to be in on this, and I want it real quick. I'll make a statement he can film, do all his bullshit with, and I'll produce evidence. Then you and Parker can strike a deal for me. I'll be long gone and the understanding I want is just that I won't be pursued. Ever.'

I had trouble keeping a straight face. 'Parker.'

He drained the glass and when he saw it was empty his hands began to shake. He said, 'Fuck it,' and reached into his jacket pocket. He took out a metal cylinder about the size of a lipstick and a masked razor blade. He got up, grabbed a recipe book Lily had bought from above the fridge and spilled white powder from the cylinder onto its laminated surface. He constructed two lines, took a short plastic straw from his shirt pocket and snorted the lines—left nostril, right nostril. He licked his index finger, dabbed up the residue, rubbed it on his gums and tidied the fixings away.

'That'd look great on the video,' I said.

He sat and drew in several deep breaths. He blinked his eyes, moved his head from side to side and rotated his shoulders as if he was trying to speed up the effect of the drug through the upper half of his body. It seemed to work after a fashion, but only briefly.

'Don't worry,' he said. 'I'll be straight when the camera rolls.'

A smile now, almost foolish. He wagged a finger at me. 'Know how I twigged that you and Kristos were acting?'

'No idea.'

'I went to NIDA for a year. Didn't make the cut. They said I wasn't any good. Maybe I wasn't. I thought I was. Anyway, I can tell bad acting when I see it.'

'You should've stuck with it. I believe Mel Gibson didn't graduate either.'

But he wasn't listening to me, only to himself. 'I know how they work, those Internal Affairs cunts. They target you and play their fuckin' funny games long range. Frank Parker, Frankie the Clean, and Cliff Hardy, the disgraceful private eye. Both out of the action. Bullshit.

'Soon as your sheila got hit they saw their chance and moved in on us. Got to Kristos. Save the wog and fuck the rest of us. Fuck, I should've seen it coming. It was all too good to last. Mind you, I was only in on the drugs and that, not the big bucks, not the killings or the cover-ups. You have to believe me, Hardy.'

'It doesn't matter whether I believe you or not. Your proposition's interesting. I'll put it to Townsend and … other parties. It'd take a while to set up …'

He shook his head and sniffed hard. His eyes were bright from the coke and his hands had steadied. 'Has to be tomorrow night. Sunday. Things are quiet. That's all the time I can allow. Soon as it's done, I'm out of here.'

'How do I contact you?'

He laughed. 'You're fuckin' joking. I'll contact you at intervals. That phone of yours better be to hand. I'm lying low, very low.'

'What if it can't be worked out? What d'you do then if this plan of yours falls through? Where d'you go?'

'Think I'd tell you? You'd be after me with the bolt cutters.'

'What's to stop me using them on you now to get this name?'

'I thought about that. You wouldn't kill me because that'd close the book. You might try to beat it out of me. Might succeed, but how would you know I wasn't lying?'

'How would we know that anyway, if we play along with you?'

'You'd know.'

I nodded. He was far gone in what I guessed was a mixture of fantasy and reality and there was no point in heavying him. As doped up as he was, he'd be close to oblivious to pain. Playing along was the only way ahead, although as a strategy it was as full of holes as his story.

I picked up the mobile. 'Want to hear me talk to people?'

'Fuck no. I'm going off to get some sleep. Haven't had any since … I dunno.'

'You're too wired to sleep.'

'I've got some downers.'

He heaved himself up, suddenly looking older and heavier and slower in the body, although his head was still buzzing.

'Are you going to drive like that?' I said.

'Why not? Been doing it for years. Get on the dog and bone, Hardy, if you want to find out what's really been going on.' He gave an uncharacteristically high-pitched laugh. 'That's as one thoroughly fucked-up detective to another.'

I let him out—watched him gather himself for the step, the path, the gate, the crossing of the street, the location of the keys, the remote, the car door, the ignition. He drove off, apparently in control, but I hoped for his sake, and other road-users, that his bolthole wasn't too far away.

I made coffee and turned to my notebook diagram, but there was no point in adding anything, or revising it. It hadn't been of any particular use anyway, and now the whole game had changed. I could believe that Gregory was in the grip of a fear that he was to be made the patsy by Kristos, with the cooperation of me and others. Why not? It had happened before. His offer to dump on everyone and skip away also seemed feasible. If he'd been in on drug dealing for some time, the chances were that he'd feathered his nest. His own drug use was a factor, too. Bound to have an effect on his paranoia.

But what had kicked him off? What had brought him to the point of suspecting Kristos and feeling that their whole operation was sliding out of control?

It could have been the murder of Williams. Killing journalists is one thing, risky enough in its way, but killing a police officer ups the ante. I thought of the Neddy Smith, Chris Flannery, Michael Drury quagmire that had cops and crims turning against each other like ravening wolves. But what if the trigger was something else? I didn't know enough about Gregory, but there was that little bit of his recent past I did know about. What if this break-out had something to do with Jane Farrow?

20

I rang Townsend and told him what had happened. Only thing to do.

'Jesus,' he said. 'This is getting sticky. Jane's changed her mind, wants to move now on her plan. Says she can't take the strain any longer.'

'And you told her how much?'

'Nothing, as agreed.'

'Well, let's make it all one big show—Jane, Gregory, Kristos, Perkins, the whole cast, all singing their heads off.'

'You're not serious.'

'No. You have to stall Jane. Do Gregory first. If he's got what he says he has, the whole Jane/Morello thing might not be needed.'

'You believe that, Cliff?'

'No, not really. Gregory's a close-to-the-edge cokehead, but we can't afford to pass up on what he has to say. Surely you can hold Jane off for forty-eight hours? You with your charm.'

'Fuck you again. I can. But you know what you have to do, don't you? Good luck.'

He meant I had to convince Frank Parker to play along with the scenario Gregory had devised in his disturbed mind. Not easy, with Frank still clinging to correct police procedure, despite some of his recent experiences and all the shit that he knew was going down with the Northern Crimes Unit. It wasn't something to negotiate over the phone. A face-to-face job.

I'd charged the mobile as soon as I'd got home from the lunch meeting with Townsend, so it had plenty of juice to be available for Gregory's call. I went on trusting Hank's assurance that my landline was clear and rang Frank. I told him that I needed to see him urgently and that I needed a big favour.

There was a pause at the end of the line and I could imagine Frank's mixed reactions. He hated being retired and out of the swim. He loved his wife and his son and his grandchildren, twin girls, now somewhere in the Third World. We were close friends who'd helped each other in the past and caused each other problems. It had to be lineball when it came to the important moves.

As always, Frank tried for a light touch. 'Cliff, how close are you sailing now to what might be called the waters of significant criminality?'

'Not that close, and not into the deepest waters.'

'The shallow waters are the most dangerous. Didn't you know that?'

'Frank …'

I must have struck the right note. He agreed to meet me at six thirty after he'd played squash in Edgecliff.

'Squash?' I said. 'What's wrong with tennis at White City?'

'Looks like rain.'

*

I got to the squash courts in time to watch Frank polish off the opposition in the last few points of the final game. Frank was a good tennis player. He always beat me when his mind was on the job and sometimes when it wasn't. He had a killer backhand, the stroke that was my greatest weakness, and Frank could hit to it off either wing till it broke down. I hadn't seen him play squash before—a game I hated—but he was just as good.

He farewelled his friend, mopped his face on a towel, and came over to where I sat.

'Hasn't rained,' I said. 'You'd have been better off playing a real game outside under lights.'

'I like sweating. There's a juice bar and a wet bar here. Which would you prefer?'

'Take a wild guess.'

'One of your quotes. So happens I know that one— *Midnight Run*. Good film.'

'It's films I want to talk to you about, sort of.'

We went down some steps to a tiny space fitted up like a trophy room with fake cups and plaques in glass cases, and photos of squash and tennis players, golfers and yachtsmen on the walls.

'Kitsch, I know,' Frank said. 'Beer? It's all foreign.'

'Stella, then.'

He came back with the bottles and glasses and we poured and lowered the levels. It took me a bottle before I got through everything I had to tell him about Gregory's proposal and Townsend's willingness to play along. I felt a bit guilty, but I didn't tell him about all the rest of it— Morello, Farrow—then I asked him for the favour.

'Jesus Christ, Cliff,' he said. 'This is cowboy stuff.'

'The Northern Crimes Unit's a cowboy outfit. To me, this is about Lily.'

He nodded, said nothing.

'I know it sounds weird, but all you have to do is act a bit. Must've done that in your time, Frank. Have to admit it's interesting.'

'I wish I could be confident you've told me everything.'

I drained my glass. 'Everything you need to know, mate. Another?'

'Why not? Okay, I'm in.'

The mobile phones got a workout over the next twenty-four as we arranged to meet Gregory in Blakehurst. The deal was that he'd take up a position some distance from the actual meeting place and observe the arrival of Townsend, Parker and me in a single vehicle—mine. When he was satisfied we weren't being followed or had an entourage, he'd advise us of the next step.

I collected the other two in Leichhardt. Townsend had his recorder, I had the .45; Frank's contribution was three kevlon vests.

I said, 'How the hell did you get these?'

'I called in a favour,' Frank said. 'I'm fast running out of them, but Gregory's bound to have a weapon. And from your account of his state of mind it seems like a sensible precaution.'

Townsend put his vest on with apparent enjoyment. He'd obviously worn these things before. I hadn't, and struggled with the straps. Clearly, Townsend was impressed by Parker's steadiness. He could probably detect a faint smell of whisky from me, very faint. With Townsend in the front and Parker in the back, I drove towards checkpoint number one.

'He's cautious,' Townsend said. 'Like you in Drummoyne, Cliff.'

Parker said, 'He's experienced. Vince Gregory had a pretty good record before he went into the Northern Crimes Unit. Some good results.'

We reached the checkpoint and stopped. Waited. After ten minutes my mobile rang.

'Hardy? Got Townsend and Parker with you?'

He could probably see us, or was bluffing that he could. But he was scripting the scene for now, and I played along.

'Yes, they're here.'

'Right. The caravan park. Stop at the gates and wait. I'll tell you the cabin number when I'm ready. Approach on foot.'

He sounded composed. In one way that was good, not in another.

'Have you got a gun?' I asked before he could cut the connection.

'Bet your fuckin' life I've got a gun. Several, and I'll use them if I have to.'

The phone went dead. 'He's heavily armed,' I said. 'But he doesn't sound wired.'

Parker said, 'It's not too late to call this off. He's down there somewhere and he's got drugs and guns he shouldn't have. I could call it in, and we could take him as he is.'

'We'd get nothing but bullshit, Frank. And if they locked him up you know the others'd find a way to get to him. He says he can tell me who killed Lily. That's my focus. You said you were in.'

'I am,' Parker said, 'just spelling it out for you. Townsend?'

'I don't know how much Cliff's told you, Mr Parker, but it's more than just a story for me. It's personal as well. Bit like Cliff. Not exactly, but …'

'Bugger you both,' Parker said. 'Let's get to this bloody caravan park and play it by ear.'

Townsend had the UBD on his lap and a small torch in his hand. 'It's down near the water as you'd expect,' he said. 'First left, second right.'

A boom gate barred the entrance to the caravan park. Presumably the occupants had means of opening it. A few lights were on inside the area, but at this time of year there wouldn't be many transients. Hard to tell how many residents. We sat in the car and did some more waiting. The sky was cloudy but cleared to reveal a bright moon. The Georges River water was calm, with no breeze blowing. The lights of Tom Ugly's bridge were reflected in the water; the sounds of the traffic carried clearly and the car lights gave the scene its only movement. The stillness tested my nerves.

The mobile beeped and I answered.

'Cabin twelve,' Gregory said. 'Set off in ten minutes.'

'Where is it?'

'A hundred metres down, bear right. There's an overhead light. You'll find it.'

I told the others what he'd said.

'Bugger that,' Frank said. 'Don't let him call all the shots.'

We got out of the car and approached the boom gate. Frank and I ducked under it.

'Shit,' Townsend said. 'I need a backup battery. Hang on a minute.'

He returned to the car, not moving any more quickly than he had to. I heard Frank give an exasperated chuckle.

'He's dancing to Gregory's tune. Doesn't want to upset him.'

'He's going okay though, wouldn't you say?'

'I don't know,' Frank said. 'There's a lot I don't like about this.'

Townsend took his time. He rejoined us without speaking and we walked down the gravel road. As my eyes adjusted to the shadows, I saw that the lights showing were mostly in cabins away to the left, towards the water. Gregory's instructions were taking us in the opposite direction. A thick cloud obscured the moon just then and visibility dropped suddenly.

I hadn't realised it, but Frank and I, tall men, were striding, and Lee Townsend was almost trotting to keep up. Typically, he made no protest. When we were well down the road, a light showed off to the right. A cabin stood in a space mostly set up for transients' caravans and vehicles.

'Has to be it,' Townsend said.

We stopped as Frank extended an arm to keep us back. He appeared to be sniffing the air.

'What?' I said.

The quiet and stillness were blasted by the roar of an engine. A motorbike. No lights, just the shattering sound receding as we stood there, helpless in the dark.

21

The noise of the motorbike didn't spark any alarm inside the caravan park. Perhaps the residents were used to hoons disturbing the peace at night. We ran to cabin number twelve. There were lights on inside and the front door was open. Townsend, the youngest and fittest, got there first and barged in. The cabin was a one-room job— a sitting space, a bed, a kitchenette. The television was on with the sound muted, a fast food ad showing.

Vince Gregory sat facing the television. His eyes were open but he wasn't seeing anything. He wore a white shirt and the collar and shoulder on the right side were dark with blood. His left arm had flopped down beside the chair. I felt for a pulse but there was nothing. Townsend unzipped his briefcase and took out his recorder.

'Don't,' Frank said.

Townsend froze. 'Why not?'

'Just don't.'

Frank gestured for us to go outside and we did. He took out his mobile and stabbed the buttons. He gave his name, the location, reported the discovery of a body and agreed to remain where he was.

'Jesus,' Townsend said, 'at least let's have a look around. He was supposed to have evidence that—'

'You really think it'd still be here, Lee?' I said.

'It could be.'

'You go in there and start poking about,' Frank said, 'and you'll leave fingerprints and DNA all over the place. We're going to have a hard enough time explaining what we're doing here without that.'

'At least let me get a picture.'

'No. The man was a police officer. Show some respect.'

'Police officer my arse. He was a criminal.'

Frank took a step and loomed over him. 'You're a one-man court of law, are you? You'll stay here and shut up until the police arrive. Then you can say what you like.'

In that mood Frank Parker could be pretty intimidating, but Townsend wasn't cowed. He swore, swung away and made a call on his mobile. His voice was urgent, demanding—the little man with the big presence. From what I heard, I gathered he was contacting his lawyer. It looked as if I'd have to call on the services of Viv Garner yet again.

The uniforms arrived first, then the detectives, then the forensic team. By this time the caravan park was well awake with people in their dressing gowns and slippers taking an interest and the resident manager, hastily dressed, talking to the police. Frank and I said we'd make statements at the right time under the right conditions. Townsend refused to say a word until his solicitor was by his side. The cops treated Frank with respect in deference to his former rank. Townsend got the treatment appropriate to a medium-ranked celebrity. It was only Frank's presence that stopped them treating me like shit. If they'd known I had an un-licensed pistol in the pocket of my denim jacket they might've done it anyway.

They said my car would be impounded. I handed over the keys. They bundled us into two of their vehicles—Frank in one, Townsend and me in the other—and took us to their HQ in Hurstville. Of course they found the .45 and confiscated my mobile. I took off the bulletproof vest and surrendered it. The others did the same. They put us in separate rooms.

I prepared myself for a long and difficult night. The interview room was typically bleak—fluorescent light, no windows, plastic chairs, nondescript table, stand and plugs for recording equipment, and that was it. I draped my jacket over the back of one chair to give it a bit of padding, pulled another one over as a leg rest and stretched back and out as best I could. Nothing to read, nothing to eat or drink, nothing to do but think. Not the Lubianka or Guantanamo Bay, but bad enough to be going on with.

As I sat there with my bones aching, my stomach growling and the need for a piss building, one thing was clear. Someone within the Northern Crimes Unit, or in the employ of someone within it, had learned of Gregory's defection and taken steps to frustrate it. Very effective steps bearing the hallmark of two of the three earlier killings—the neat, one low-calibre bullet execution. That was the person I needed to find. We'd never know now whether Gregory had the name and the evidence to back it up.

Another thing. Whoever had got to Gregory had waited until he'd identified his visitors. I could hear Gregory's voice on the phone: *Hardy? Got Townsend and Parker with you?*

Not a comfortable feeling. He was out there, killing policemen, the most serious crime of all in the eyes of many.

Midnight came and went and then it got weird. The door opened and a uniformed female constable beckoned me out and asked, not told, me to follow her. I went along a passage and up some stairs. She opened a door and ushered me in. Different setting altogether—carpet, windows, easy chairs, civilised lighting. Frank and Townsend, both nursing coffee cups, sat a little apart and two men in suits sat nearby—one middle-aged, fattish, fair; the other younger, dark. Suits but no ties, stubble—called out in the early hours.

Lawyers? I thought. *No. Cops, senior cops.*

Frank stood and did the introductions. 'Cliff, this is Senior Superintendent Matthews and Superintendent Mattioli.'

Matthews gestured towards a coffee machine and cups sitting on top of a bar fridge. 'Have some coffee, Mr Hardy.'

'Tell you the truth, I'd rather have a piss.'

Matthews said, 'Constable.'

The uniformed woman was standing with her back to the door. She opened it and I went through. Before the door closed I heard Matthews say quietly, 'I hope he isn't going to be difficult.' Must have known a bit about me.

I pissed, washed my hands and face, felt better. Back in the room, I poured myself a cup of coffee, drained it in one go, poured another, sat down. Matthews dismissed the underling and cleared his throat.

'My colleague and I are from the Internal Affairs Division, Mr Hardy. When Mr Parker had spoken to the

Hurstville detectives we were contacted, and that's why you and Mr Townsend are at this meeting.'

I sipped the less than hot coffee. Didn't speak.

Mattioli picked up the ball. 'We've had an interest in the Northern Crimes Unit for some time. We have intelligence on a number of officers, especially Gregory.'

No rank, surname only—getting ready to have him carry the can?

I glanced at Frank, whose nod told me to hear the man out.

The two of them, playing good cop and better cop, went on for a while about the intelligence they'd gathered on the unit and their plan to conduct investigations of, and mount surveillance on, some of its members. That plan was still part of their agenda, although the night's events had thrown a spanner in the works.

'We want your cooperation,' Matthews said, including Frank and Townsend by inclining his head towards them, 'in keeping a lid on what happened tonight as much as possible.'

I could hardly stop myself from laughing—it tends to happen when I hear bureaucrats talking about 'intelligence' —but I kept a straight face.

'I'm listening,' I said.

Mattioli said, 'We know you have a personal interest in—'

'So does Pamela Williams,' I said, 'and someone else I won't name. And—who knows?—maybe someone cared for Rex Robinson. Not likely, from what I'm told, but possible. Are you going to go along with this shit, Frank? Lee?'

Townsend looked at the floor as if the pattern in the carpet was of intense interest. Frank stared at me. We'd known each other for a long time and been at the barricades together. He could read me and I could read him. He opened his hands, hot gospel preacher-style.

'They've got us on all sorts of counts, Cliff—conspiracy for one. The prohibited equipment—the vests, plus your pistol—give them the terrorism angle if they want to use it. My pension could be at risk and Townsend's whole career. It's a lay-down misère.'

Frank knew how much I hated card games and how hopeless I was at them. But his message was clear—don't stir, not now.

'Okay,' I said. 'I might play along if I hear a bit more.'

Matthews said the other senior members of the Northern Crimes Unit would be called in for questioning and that their activities and finances would be subject to intense investigation.

'They'll be spooked,' I said. 'They'll run for cover.'

Matthews smiled. 'I understand you were a boxer, Mr Hardy. What did Joe Louis say about … whoever it was?'

'It's pronounced Lewis, not Louey,' I said, 'and it was Billy Coon. Joe said, "He can run, but he can't hide".'

Matthews wasn't the least put out by my one-upmanship. 'Exactly,' he went on. 'We'll have two objects. One, to discover the connection between police officers and the deaths of the people Mr Hardy has referred to, and that of Inspector Gregory, of course. Two, to bring to an end the criminality that seems to have prevailed under the protection, possibly with the connivance of …'

'Of?' I said.

Mattioli said, 'That remains to be determined.'

Townsend spoke for the first time since I'd come into the room. No knowing what had gone down beforehand. 'I noticed that the police at the caravan park kept the media at a distance. D'you think you can sit on this?'

'We'll try,' Matthews said, 'with your cooperation.'

The soft soap approach. I wondered where Townsend's lawyer was. I also wondered whether Townsend had been given a chance, or had wanted, to talk to Frank about Farrow's plan and the Morello photographs. Probably not. My guess was that he'd opt to keep exploiting the evidence we had—and the people involved.

'Cliff?' Frank said.

I looked directly at Matthews, taking in the double chin, the stomach bulge over the belt slung below his gut. A self-indulgent man, but not a stupid one. A dangerous combination.

'What's our role in your ongoing investigation?' I said, trying to keep the sarcasm out of my voice but probably not succeeding. Matthews was tired; Mattioli was angry; Frank was resigned; Townsend showed no reaction.

'Consultative,' Matthews said.

I said, 'What does that mean?'

Matthews scratched at a patch of stubble near his bottom lip that was irritating him, but not as much as I was. 'Hardy,' he said, 'it means whatever the fuck I want it to mean.'

22

The same policewoman escorted us from the building. My keys had been returned and my car stood immediately outside the police station. They hadn't returned my gun or the vests. Without speaking, we got in the car and I drove to Leichhardt where I'd picked up Frank and Townsend. Silence all the way. Private thoughts.

'Sorry for the trouble, Frank,' I said when I stopped. 'Didn't work out quite as we planned.'

Frank opened the door. 'Things seldom do, Cliff. But it worked out worse for Vince Gregory than for us.' He reached over and patted my shoulder. 'Take my advice and keep clear of it.'

'You know I can't do that.'

'I know, but I had to say it anyway. Those two reckon they'll keep me informed. I doubt it, but anything I hear I'll pass on.'

'They're looking to pin the murders on Gregory and do a bit of housekeeping and that'll be it,' Townsend said.

Frank got out of the car. 'Maybe. I'll be in touch, Cliff.'

He walked to his car, opened it with the remote, and drove away. Townsend stayed where he was in the back.

'This is all bullshit,' he said.

'What is?'

'Them saying they'll look into the finances, their fucking close investigation in inverted commas. It'll be a cover-up.'

'Right.'

'So you're not going to play along?'

'Of course not. Frank knows I won't. Did you hear anything of the discussion between him and Matthews and Mattioli?'

'No. They seemed to have settled things before they brought me in, but *I* was told I wouldn't be detained or charged and that I could call off my solicitor. So I did.'

'And what did you tell them about Jane Farrow and Hannah Morello?'

'Are you nuts? I told them fucking nothing.'

'So we're still after Perkins and Kristos with our original leverage. Vince Gregory was a … distraction.'

'Jesus, Hardy, that's a bit harsh.'

I swivelled around and looked at him. 'Gregory called you the poor man's John Pilger.'

Townsend laughed, then stifled the sound. 'I'm flattered, I think.' At that moment he sounded tired. 'What's the point?'

'The point is, I don't care about Gregory or your feelings or sensitivities. I'm going where I've always been going—to whoever killed Lily, and I'll use you and Jane Farrow and Hannah Morello and anyone else to get there.'

'I understand.'

'Do you? I want to carry through with Jane's plan ASAP.'

Townsend apparently felt at a disadvantage sitting in the back of the car. Vertically challenged as he was, he'd feel at a disadvantage sitting anywhere. He got out quickly and came around to my half-lowered window, taking the higher ground.

'I can't see that working,' he said. 'The NCU's bound to be in an uproar. Anyway, her strategy was to work through Gregory and he's dead.'

His use of the acronym annoyed me. I was strung out from the frustration of the night's events. 'Fuck that,' I said. 'She switches her focus to Perkins.'

'I'm not sure she'd—'

'She carries through on it or I tell Perkins and Kristos she's an informer and that we've got evidence from her of what's been going on and who's in the shit and we see where the chips fall.'

He backed off a step. 'You wouldn't.'

'Try me.'

I started the engine and pulled away with minimum acceleration. He took a couple of steps as if he wanted to stop me, but he pulled up. I watched him for a few seconds—growing smaller in the rear vision mirror.

I meant it at the time, but I'm not sure I could've carried it through. The odds against it working were pretty long, and the chance that Farrow would finish up dead were good. Someone in the picture was, or had the use of, an unscrupulous killer, and one dead police person more or less wouldn't make much difference. It hadn't needed spelling out to Frank and Townsend that we were all in danger from this person, if not immediately then later, depending on how things worked out.

Frank and I could take care of ourselves and I had no doubt Townsend could arrange protection. Besides, now I had house security—not as good as his, but good enough. But maybe the smart play was to let the Internal Affairs people have their way and tackle Perkins and Kristos later when they were demoted, suspended or cut loose, if that's what happened.

The morning paper had a brief, ill-informed report on a man murdered in Blakehurst. I spent most of Monday cleaning out the Newtown office and convincing myself that sitting tight was the right thing to do. It was a wet, dreary day and my mood deteriorated with the weather. Handling old case files wasn't calculated to improve things. I'd meant to throw a lot of this stuff away when I'd moved from Darlinghurst but somehow I hadn't got around to it. I knew there were some things I wanted to keep and I couldn't find the will to do the sorting. Seemed easier just to bundle it all up and stick it out of sight.

Same thing now. *Why not heave it all?* I thought, but I knew I wouldn't. Over the years I'd handled hundreds of cases, mostly small, some medium, a few large. There was no pattern to the outcomes, which varied between success, stalemate and failure. As I reached into the back of the lowest drawer of the filing cabinet, the one that always stuck after I'd once kicked it shut in a display of temper, I felt something unusual, unexpected, behind the last bunch of folders I'd left in the cardboard box I'd used to transport them. I pushed the folders out of the way and scrabbled in the back of the box. What I came up with was a bundle in plastic wrapping so old it had gone dry and crisp.

I knew what it was, although I didn't like to think how long it had been since I'd put it there and completely forgotten about it—a long time, much water under many bridges. Soon after I'd opened my office, a woman had come in and tried to hire me to shoot her husband. She had the gun for the job—a Walther P38. She was in a distraught state over her husband's infidelity. I calmed her down and persuaded her there were better ways of getting even. I introduced her to a lawyer who shepherded her through a divorce that netted her a solid percentage of the husband's considerable fortune. I kept the gun, wrapped it up in a couple of plastic bags, shoved it in a box and forgot about it.

The plastic came away easily and the gun was still in good condition as far as I could tell. No rust and the magazine released easily. I expelled the bullets, which also seemed to be as good as new. I doubted that the pistol had ever been fired. How she got hold of it I never knew. I worked the action a few times and it seemed free. I had cleaning equipment at home. What's a private detective without a gun? Except that I wasn't a private detective any longer. I put the Walther in the pocket of my leather jacket, zipped it up tight.

I carted the boxes of files and other things like the coffee maker, the fax machine and the computer and printer back to Glebe and installed the useful bits in the spare room. The files stayed in boxes on the floor. After watching the news—nothing on Gregory—and eating something, I poured a glass of red and amused myself by cleaning the pistol. I was putting off ringing Townsend for an update on Jane Farrow. I'd had a few glasses and was feeling the effects. I thought about my once-legitimate .38 revolver and the illicit .45 automatic and a bit of the Oscar Wilde line popped into my head, with a variation: *To lose one pistol, Mr Hardy ...*

I was smiling at my own wit when the door buzzer sounded. I assembled the pistol and went to the door. The peephole showed me Lee Townsend standing back so that

I could see most of him. Townsend, the short-arse, knew better than to stand close up.

I opened the door, holding the pistol behind my back. He was carrying a bottle. Shaped up as a better guest than I was a host. He came in and saw the gun.

'Jesus Christ, Cliff. What're you expecting?'

I laughed. 'I was cleaning it. I was going to ring you but now you're here.'

'You've had a few.'

'Ready for a few more. What's that you've got there?'

'Wolf Blass. We have to talk.'

'Right. Through here.'

I led him to the kitchen and handed him the corkscrew, always to hand. 'Crack it. I'll get the glasses.'

To do him credit, he didn't make a survey of the sixties decor or the much earlier structural decay. He opened the bottle with an expert touch. I got two glasses and we perched on either side of the bench. I put the gun on the sink and poured.

Townsend drank half the glass in a gulp. 'Have you been married, Cliff? Or lived with women? Other than Lily, I mean.'

The wine was several notches better than the stuff I'd been drinking. I sipped it. 'Yeah, two or three.'

'Did you ever think you'd made one happy?'

It wasn't what I wanted to talk about, but something in his manner made me respond. I thought about Cyn, Helen Broadway, Glen Withers ...

'No,' I said, 'not really.'

'Why was that?'

'Not sure. Partly to do with me, I guess, the way I am. But I don't think the women I've been with had a great capacity for happiness. Not many women do.'

'Just women?'

I supposed this was leading to Jane Farrow by a round-about route so I went along with it, although philosophising wasn't my strong suit. 'I think men achieve it more easily, at least for some of the time, from what they do. With women, it seems to be harder. This's partly the wine talking. Where's this going, Lee?'

He drained his glass as if he was trying to catch up with me. I poured him some more.

'Jane tore strips off me when she heard about what she called our cowboy show last night.'

'That shouldn't surprise you.'

'No, what surprised me was some of the things she said about ... well, us. I mean, there was mutual attraction, sure. And good sex. But I thought her real interest in me was closely tied in with what I could do for her. But it turned out she was more on about how disappointed she was that I hadn't trusted her and had gone behind her back and shaken the feelings she was starting to have for me. Coming from someone like her, I tell you it cut through.'

I nodded and we both drank some more wine.

He went on, 'I got defensive, angry, upset. She wanted to know how it was we weren't charged and how there was nothing much in the media.'

'What did you say?'

'I was tempted to tell her the truth, but my back was up and I lied. I said that Parker had used his influence as a former deputy commissioner to get us off the hook and the police had given the media bugger-all. She seemed to accept that.'

'Good.'

'We were at my place. We both calmed down and sort of apologised and we ended up in bed.'

'Good luck to you. When was this?'

'This afternoon. She had the day off. The thing is, she wants to go ahead with her plan, and just the way you suggested—targeting Perkins. And she wants to do it soon.

23

I could think of a number of theoretical objections to the plan, but remembering the character of Jane Farrow, I knew that none of them would sway her. If she was determined to go ahead, that was fine with me and the thing for Townsend and me to do was offer her as much support as we could and look to satisfy our own needs—for me, justice for Lily's death, for Townsend, a big story and, possibly, the saving of his relationship with Farrow.

I said these things, more or less, as we finished off the bottle of wine. For a small man, Townsend appeared to hold his grog well. He was determined to drive home so I got out some biscuits and cheese as blotter and brewed coffee.

'How soon's soon?' I asked.

'She says a couple of days.'

'Can you set things up that quickly? You told her it'd take a week. It'll be a rush but she's calling the shots.'

'Hmm ... First I have to know the meeting place. She says she'll try to make it somewhere people can hide.'

'Their people or ours?'

'That's one of the problems, isn't it?'

'It could be. When d'you expect her to get back to you on that?'

Townsend shrugged. 'With her, who knows? She's an alpha female. There's a bit more I have to tell you.'

I told him to have something to eat and to drink some coffee before he did. Gave me time to anticipate what it might be. Difficult to see how things could be more uncertain or dangerous.

He cleared his throat. 'After we'd … reconciled, I showed her the little Morello video and told her about the photographs.'

He obviously expected me to explode and, maybe if I hadn't had so much to drink, I would have. But for an aggressive, assertive man, he was now showing a vulnerability I hadn't seen before and I didn't have the heart to make it any harder, at least until I'd heard him out. *Stay calm*, I told myself.

'That's without showing the face of the woman or using her name, right?'

Relief showed in his every movement as he drank more coffee. 'Yes, of course.'

I felt I'd been too soft. 'It wasn't a fucking rhetorical question. Did you or didn't you use the name, let it slip between kisses?'

'I did not.'

'Okay. Well, in a way it puts the matter into an interesting perspective. Did you tell her I had the photos?'

'No, but she knows we're working together and …'

'Right. So if anyone comes after me or you in the next couple of days, we'll know she's playing for the other side, won't we?'

He went pale, almost yellow under my spotty light. 'I didn't think of that.'

'Have to think of everything. Cheer up—you've got good security and so have I. Just keep a wary eye out.'

Some of the self-confidence was back. 'You're making fun of me.'

'Just a bit. Look on the bright side, Lee. If we don't get any flak coming our way you'll know we can trust her to do what she says she's going to do. Isn't that a comfort?'

'Anyone ever told you what a prick you are?'

'Just a few.'

Townsend went home and I cleaned up, put the pistol away and went to bed. I woke up in the early hours zooming out of a fierce nightmare. One of those that make you relieved that you're awake, at home and still alive. I've heard that the part of the brain that produces nightmares is the same part that affects schizophrenics. If that's true, their pain and fear must be truly terrible.

The experience left me too shaken to get back to sleep. I tried to read Doctorow's book about Sherman's march through Georgia. Great stuff, but I couldn't concentrate and some of it was too bleak for my mood. I got up, made coffee, ate two boiled eggs and moved restlessly from one room to another. Wandering about in an empty house in the early hours of a soon-to-be winter morning isn't good preparation for confident forward planning. I worried about where things stood with Townsend and Farrow and the Northern Crimes Unit and the Internal Affairs people. Complicated. Twisted.

Pieces of the nightmare came back to me the way they can after the event. It had something to do with a threat to my daughter Megan as a child. Not a lot of sense in that, because I didn't meet her until she was past adolescence. But perhaps that was the source of the mental disturbance. Trouble was, she seemed to have a blind brother and that made no sense at all.

Dawn and the opportunity to go up the road for the papers came as a relief. It was drizzling. I pulled on a plastic raincoat with a hood and I was about to leave the house when the thought struck me that Jane Farrow had had plenty of time to relay the information about the Morello evidence, if that was the game she was playing. I put the Walther in my pocket.

Nothing happened, except my feet got wet in leaky sneakers. I read the papers. Still no significant coverage of Gregory's death. It was being sat on very effectively. Mid-morning the phone rang.

'Hardy.'

'Mr Hardy, this is Hannah Morello.'

I had a full cup of coffee in my hand and I spilled some. 'What's wrong?'

'Nothing. Why should anything be wrong?'

'I'm sorry. That's good. What can I do for you?'

'Oh no, you can't brush me off like that. What's been happening?'

I gave her an abbreviated version of events, stressing that no mention had been made of her in the proceedings.

'You didn't sound so sure of that when I said who I was.'

'It's at an edgy stage, Mrs Morello. I couldn't see how you'd be in danger, and I'm glad you're not alarmed. Townsend and I could be in the firing line. We'll have to wait and see. Now, what was it?'

'I don't suppose you know the school holidays have started.'

'I didn't, no.'

'There speaks the childless man. Well, they have, and I got a call from Pam in Rockhampton. She's fine. She's settled in with her sister. Apparently they've got a big place and she wants me and the kids to come up and stay for a while.'

'Sounds good. Rocky'd be better than down here at this time of year.'

'Milly and Josh're dead keen and I could do with a break. I just wondered if I was going to be needed while you go about nailing those bastards.'

'Maybe later if the photographs need to be verified, but for now …'

'Given you're not a hundred per cent sure I'd be safe, going to Queensland would be a bloody good idea. Thank you, Mr Hardy.'

She rang off. Not entirely pleased. Couldn't blame her, but at least one niggling area of worry was out of the way. There were plenty more to be going on with.

I went to the gym, parked where I had the night I was attacked, and got through a pretty solid workout. A few people I knew were there and we yarned in between sets and cracked the usual gym jokes.

Heard about aerobics in hell?

No.

Starts with ten million leg lifts.

I enjoyed the companionship and felt my mood, which had been dark ever since Lily died, begin to lift a bit. I felt so good physically that I even did some stretching. Not much.

With the coldness of the day, a hot spa appealed and I soaked in the bubbles for a full cycle. I passed on the sauna—enough is enough. I wandered down to the Bar Napoli and had a flat white. At one time, when I had a second generation Italian offsider named Scott Galvani, I acquired a smattering of Italian. I'd lost it, but it was good to hear the language being spoken around me and to pick up a word or two. I'd been to Italy once, very briefly, liked it a lot. Looking at the wall posters—the standard stuff: the Colosseum, Pompeii, the Isle of Capri—I thought I'd like to see it again, closer up and for longer. I realised that I was looking ahead, beyond settling accounts for Lily.

The drizzle had stopped but the day was overcast with more rain predicted. I walked back to my car parking spot and was about to open the door when I heard a shout from somewhere above me.

'Hey!'

The memory of the attack here and my army training and long experience kicked in, and I had the pistol out of the raincoat pocket and was crouched down with the car for cover before the sound of the shout had died away. I looked up and saw a man leaning out of a window, well above me and to my left. He was in his pyjamas and had a stubbie in his hand. I lowered the pistol and stood.

'What?' I said.

'I seen you here last week when you got attacked, like. You all right?'

'Yeah.'

'That's thanks to me, mate. That bugger was going to do you. I yelled at him and he pissed off.'

The window was in a building about ten metres away. I approached it. 'Well, thanks. What happened next?'

'Like I say, he shot through and I was going to call the police and that. Couldn't find me phone. Tell you the truth I was a bit pissed. I found the mobile and took another look out and you was up and moving and looked like you was gonna live, so I didn't do nothin'. Glad to see you's all right.'

He reached up to close the window but I raised a hand to stop him. 'Hold on. Did you get a good look at the guy who attacked me?'

'Yeah, mate. Pretty good.'

'Big, dark bloke in a suit, right?'

'Shit, no. He was littler than you but he musta been strong the way he grabbed you. Sort of medium-sized solid bastard. Bald head.'

'Drove off, did he? What sort of car?'

'Jesus, now you're asking. Hey, this isn't police stuff, is it, 'cos I …?'

'Nothing like that.' I opened my wallet and took out a twenty and a ten, all I had. I bent, put them on the ground and pinned them down with loose piece of concrete.

'This is yours and I'm gone as soon as you tell me about the car.'

'No car, mate. He went off on a fuckin' motorbike, and don't expect me to tell you what kind because I don't know one from another.'

My informant wasn't a witness who'd stand up in court. By his own admission he was drunk when he saw what he saw. But that didn't matter to me. His description fitted the man who'd been with Kristos at the murder of Robinson as caught on film by Danny Morello, and his departure by motorbike was too much of a coincidence not to connect it with Gregory's murder.

You don't comb Sydney for medium-sized, strong men covering their baldness with a cap and driving a motorbike. But now I had a credible description of the man who'd probably killed Lily. I looked forward to finding out who he was and to meeting him.

24

I couldn't wait any longer. If I could get hold of Kristos I'd find a way to make him tell me who his bald-headed killer mate was and all this farting about with Perkins and videos could stop right there. I had a few persuaders—the photos, kept in a deep slit in the driver's seat of the car, the Walther and a Swiss army knife. Whatever it took. I had Jane Farrows's mobile number and I rang it. She answered.

'This is Hardy. Is Kristos there?'

'No, he's been suspended along with the other senior men. What—?'

'Where does he live?'

She kept her voice low. 'What're you on about? Hasn't Lee told you we've—?'

'I don't care about that. Where does he fucking well live?'

'You'll spoil everything.'

'Where are you?'

'At my desk.'

'If you don't tell me where he lives I'm coming over there and I'll do damage to anyone who tries to stop me finding out what I need to know.'

'He lives in a flat across the road from the station here in Longueville. He's probably there now. He was in collecting stuff not long ago.'

'The exact address.'

She gave it, then she said, 'You're an arsehole, Hardy. I was talking to Lee just a little while ago. We're setting up the meeting with Perkins for tomorrow. You're going to fuck it up.'

'I don't care about your meeting or about you or Lee, but I'll tell you this, if you alert Kristos that I'm after him you'll be very sorry.'

'Fuck you.'

Had to admire her. Oddly, her resilience calmed me down. 'Listen, Jane, I reckon I've got the highest stake in this and there's a move I have to make now. Maybe I can do it so it doesn't blow your plans. I will if I can. Just sit tight and don't tell Lee about this. Go on with your arrangements. It might work out—'

She hung up on me; the second woman to do it in one day. Maybe a record.

I was calm but seething inside. I had no precise idea of how to handle Kristos, but sometimes improvisation is the best policy. It started to rain and the traffic slowed, increasing my impatience. The rain got heavier and my wipers struggled to cope. I had to concentrate to drive safely, and I had the additional worry that the petrol gauge was low. To run dry in the rain in the middle of slow-moving traffic would be no joke. It was stop-start all the way over the Harbour Bridge and through North Sydney and Greenwich—a drain on the fuel.

By Northwood the rain had stopped and, with the needle flickering below empty, I found a service station. I was about to use the pump when I remembered that I'd left the only cash I had back in the car park. I had a keycard, but I suspected that the account was just about tapped out. I put in twenty dollars worth, which gets you bugger-all these days, and asked for thirty dollars on top hoping the card would support it. It did, but it must have been a near thing.

I got on the road again and immediately lost myself. This was unfamiliar territory to me. The police had brought me to Longueville after I'd reported the Williams killing, and a taxi had taken me back to Milsons Point. I hadn't paid any attention to the route on either trip. I remembered William Hurt's line in *Body Heat*: *Sometimes the shit comes down so heavy I feel I ought to wear a hat.* I stopped, dug out the UBD, and plotted my way to the Northern Crimes HQ. My mood wasn't improving.

I turned into the street, looking out for a block of flats opposite the police station. It was easy to spot. Cream brick, three storey, pebbles and garden, balconies. I drove past and found a parking place around the corner. It felt chancy to be across from a police station, carrying a gun and about to front up aggressively to a serving, if suspended, policeman, but I was charged up enough to do it.

There were several entrances to the block and the one that led to Kristos's flat was at the front. Good security: you had to buzz from outside the building to be admitted. I pressed the buzzer for the flat number Jane Farrow had given me and waited for a response. None came. I tried again with the same result. Frustration was building as I thought I'd have to lie in wait for him to come home. I pressed again. Still nothing.

The standard trick is to press all the buttons, hope you get an answer and try to bluff your way in. I sneezed and stepped away to wipe my nose and, for no reason in particular, looked up. Kristos, casually dressed, was standing on a balcony three levels up, looking down at me with a mobile phone in his hand. A truck went past on the street and probably drowned out what I shouted up at him. Anyway, he didn't care. He closed the phone and went back into his flat.

I stood there, frustrated and angry. A man came walking briskly across the road, down the path to where I was, and pulled a small leather folder from his pocket. He held it up like a photographer with a light meter. Suit, tie, moustache, beer gut, warrant card. A cop. He stopped just short of arm's length.

'I'm from Internal Affairs, Hardy. You are not to make contact with any member of the Northern Crimes Unit. Do you understand?'

I glanced up. Kristos was back on his balcony, leaning on the rail, watching us.

Fall over, you bastard, I thought.

'What if he wants to see me?'

The cop shook his head. 'Do you take yourself out of here right now, or do I arrest you?'

'What for?'

'I'll think of something.'

I looked up again. Kristos had gone.

'I'm going,' I said. 'Give my regards to M and M.'

'What?'

'Matthews and Mattioli.'

I pushed past, forcing him to step into a garden bed and muddy his shiny shoes. Petty, but satisfying. Back on the street I looked across at the Northern Crimes Unit HQ with two thoughts in my mind: *Had Jane Farrow alerted Kristos? And was Internal Affairs keeping Kristos under some form of house arrest?*

The sky had cleared and the breeze was light. I went back to the car, dumped the raincoat and the pistol, and went for a walk to find a pub. There's no let-down like an anticlimax and I'd been all primed to give Kristos hell. The frustration needed working out and I couldn't think of a better way to do it than to walk and drink. Longueville is a small peninsula leading down to the Lane Cove River. Good views of the water from the high points and some of the residents and flat-builders had gone up high to make sure they got them. It took a few twists and turns, but I came upon a pub that still looked vaguely the way pubs used to look, except for the pokies.

I bought a pint of draught Guinness and a packet of chips and settled down in a corner well away from the few other drinkers in the bar. I sank half the pint in a couple of long pulls and prepared to linger over the rest—to let it soothe me as it no doubt had my Galway ancestors going way, way back.

The way things were, it looked as if Jane Farrow's plan would have to be on the agenda. There were two question marks over that. If Perkins was under the same protection or confinement as Kristos, how would she get him to a location where the whole sticky business could be carried out? Apart from that, was Farrow playing for our side or theirs? Kristos had spoken to someone to sic the Internal Affairs guy onto me. Who?

She'd said on the phone that arrangements had been made with Townsend to set up the meeting with Perkins for the following night. That was before my intervention, but I couldn't see how that would make any difference. It was time to talk to Townsend, to make a judgement on Farrow and her plan. I finished the stout and the chips, called Townsend on my mobile, found him at home and told him I was coming over. He didn't even ask why. Was that strange? I was finding many more questions than answers.

Townsend received me cheerfully at the door and we went through to his spotless, well-appointed kitchen. He offered me coffee. I accepted. He seemed relaxed and I commented on it.

'Why not?' he said.

'You're about to mount a covert operation of a sort on a senior police officer who's in collusion with a multiple killer. Plus your girlfriend will be right in the firing line. I'd have expected a little more tension.'

'Before I answer, tell me why you're here.'

I told him about my day—the happy news about Hannah Morello's holiday in the sunshine state, about the good description of the possible killer, and my failed attempt to confront Kristos.

I said, 'Has Jane spoken to you about that?'

'No, why would she know about it?'

'She'd know if she was the one who alerted Kristos that I was coming. I told her I was.'

'I haven't heard anything of this. Setting a trap, were you? You still don't trust her.'

The coffee was good and I was tired after the day's comings and goings. I drained the cup and he poured me some more—black with sugar.

'Trust can fuck you,' I said.

'That's one of the most cynical things I've ever heard, and I'm in a game where there's almost nothing but cynics.'

I shrugged.

'I'll answer your earlier question, Cliff. You don't know much about me, do you? Well, I'm older than I look. I was in Rwanda and Bosnia and Sierra Leone, and after seeing things there I got a different perspective. I mean, what happens here in Oz is a sideshow, really. Don't get me wrong, I'm happy to be here and happy to survive being close to all that civil war, ethnic cleansing shit, but it's still a sideshow.'

'What about Jane?'

'I know she's got her own agenda. No idea what it is but I trust her. No, make it that I trust my instinct about her.'

He was an experienced, perceptive man, and I had nothing solid to put up against what he was saying.

'Well, she's got the call,' I said.

'Yeah, one thing she said worries me most though. She reckons there's no way she can nominate the meeting place. Perkins'll have the say on that.'

'Can't see how that'll work.'

'Jane says she'll have a veto and they'll have to negotiate. She says she'll rule out obviously dangerous places, but we'll have to settle for the least worst.'

That 'we' almost amused me. By 'we' he didn't mean him and me, he meant him and Jane. It reminded me of the way boxing managers talk about their fighters' performances, and the famous line from manager Joe Jacobs after his fighter, Max Schmelling, lost to Jack Sharkey in a notorious home-town decision: 'We wuz robbed. We shoulda stood in bed.'

I asked him about the technical details and he said that Jane would have about her person a digital device no bigger than a pea that would pick up everything that was said over a wide range. No worries about cigarette packet-sized receivers taped to the body.

'The ... event ... meeting can be filmed with absolute clarity and soundlessly from a fair distance,' Townsend said.

'How far?'

'About a hundred metres.'

I remembered situations I'd been in when wearing a wire did involve taping something to the body with a high risk of discovery, and when remote-controlled videoing had to be done at close range and was anything but noiseless.

'Sounds all right,' I said. 'So we sit and wait for her to contact you tomorrow about the time and place?'

'That's it.'

Another evening and night to fill in, I thought. *Without Lily or the prospect of Lily.*

Townsend's mobile was on the table. I didn't recognise the ring-tone. He snatched the phone up.

'What? God! Yes, yes. Okay.'

He put the mobile down. 'It's tonight,' he said.

'Good, sooner the better. Less time for things to go wrong. What was that ring-tone?'

He was suddenly so intensely focused that my question caught him on the hop. 'What?'

'The ring-tone, what was it?'

'Why?'

'Just curious.'

'No you're not. You're just showing me how cool you can be under pressure. It's Mahler.'

'Paul Keating's favourite composer.'

'You like Mahler?'

'Lee,' I said, 'I wouldn't know Mahler from Marley.'

25

I asked the only two questions that mattered: 'Where and when?'

'Eleven thirty, Balmoral Beach.'

'Is that the best she could do?'

'Give her a break, she'd have been treading on eggshells.'

'Where precisely?'

'The rotunda. Where else?'

I tried to bring it to mind. I'd only been to the beach a few times and not recently. I seemed to remember a green belt between the road and the sea wall bordering the sand, with some sort of folly in the middle—round with white pillars. There were trees around and a building I vaguely remember—white again, and big.

'How is it for you?' I asked.

'A while since I've been there. Okay, I guess, depending on the weather.'

'Meaning?'

'High winds can interfere with the pick-up, also crashing surf.'

'It's a fucking harbour beach.'

He flared, 'Bugger you, I'm just—'

'Okay, okay, we're both on edge. I'm glad to see you're human.'

'I was wondering the same about you. I'll let you in on something—she told me not to tell you, not to bring you along.'

I laughed. 'Some chance. Where's she coming from, to say that?'

'You've rubbed her up the wrong way, obviously.'

'It's mutual. So how do we proceed?'

'I've got an offsider to handle the filming. We can't be seen to be reconnoitring, right?'

'Right.'

'But Jacques can drive by a bit earlier and look the place over. Work out where we can take up positions.'

'Jacques?'

'He's number one. Are you anti-French?'

'Hell, no. I've got a frog squatting in my family tree back there. Escaped from Devil's Island, they say. Probably bullshit. I'll go along with Jacques and drop off where I think best. He can tell *you* what to do.'

'I don't know about—'

'This is her show, your show and my show. I'm playing it my way. Lee, I've been in on sieges and ransoms and exchanges before. I think I know how to handle it.'

He sighed, looked at his Rolex. 'Okay. It's just gone eight. Plenty of time. Forty-five minutes to get there at the most. Jacques's on standby, he'll be here in a couple of minutes after I call. Is there anything you need?'

'A map'd help.'

He got on the web, Googled, and before long had a printout of information on the beach and a map. The building I only half remembered was a temple built by religious crazies in the 1920s who thought the second coming would be at Balmoral. Now it did the same job as the Bondi pavilion—changing rooms, function spaces, cafes.

'Anything else?' Townsend said.

It had been quite a few hours—not since I'd left home. 'Just a good long piss,' I said.

Jacques looked the way a Jacques is supposed to look—dark hair, eyes and skin, neat in movement and manner. His accent was Canadian, with the Scottish vowels. Townsend introduced us and we were off in his HiAce van. I asked him a few questions about the filming technique, but I didn't understand much of what he said. The night was clear and the mid-week traffic was light. He asked me to navigate. I used the UBD and small torch from the glovebox, and got us there pretty efficiently.

Even at night, the view dropping down towards the beach was dramatic, with lights on the headlands and the sea shimmering. Lights blinked on the boats moored at the small marina. We cruised along the Esplanade, the road bordering the strip of park, and then drove up a few streets until we had a view down to the beach and surroundings. The Esplanade wasn't well lit, and the big Moreton Bay figs would diminish the light in the park area. The park lights were dim. Good for some, not for others.

'What do you think?' I asked.

'Plenty of places to set up—those trees, over by the ... what is that building?'

I didn't bother with the history. 'Bathers' Pavilion.'

'There are some other spots over there. Down on the steps to the beach, or off to the right—behind that big tree with the triple trunk. What do you call it?'

'A Moreton Bay fig. Looks the best bet, wouldn't you say?'

'Yes, I think so.'

'How's the light?'

'Irrelevant, man, with the equipment I've got.'

'My eyes obviously aren't as good as yours. Have you got any night-vision glasses?'

'Of course.'

He got out, opened the side of the van and came back with field glasses as light as a feather. He made adjustments, and when I looked through them the scene was reddish-tinged but very clear.

'What's with the pistol?' Jacques said.

I'd brought the raincoat with me and the shape of the pistol in a pocket must have been plain at some point.

'Sharp eyes,' I said.

'Professional necessity. So?'

'It's more of a prop than anything else.'

'Just prop it well away from me.'

I nodded and used the glasses again, sweeping them around this time. I laughed and handed them back to him.

'What?' he said.

'Jacques, mate, this is a bloody dodgy situation all round, but there's one thing to be glad of.'

He was looking through the glasses now. 'And that is …?'

'That we're not setting up so we have to deal with that dinky little island out there.'

I'd forgotten the island although the webpage had noted it—a small outcrop reached by a stone bridge. Only a few metres out, so not really an island, but it would've added to the complications.

'You're right,' he said.

'*Bien sur.*'

'You speak French?'

'You've just heard ninety per cent of it.'

We drove down and parked a couple of hundred metres to the right of the rotunda, past the old toilet block and bush shelter, angle parking all along and there were no cars in the immediate vicinity of our target area. We established ourselves behind a Moreton Bay fig big enough to hide a caravan. Jacques phoned Townsend, who was on his way, telling him where to park. He joined us. They tinkered with their equipment while I kept watch. We had a clear view of the rotunda at about forty metres away.

Traffic on the road was sporadic and becoming more infrequent, and over the next hour lights went out in most of the apartments across the Esplanade. Immediately opposite was a school with a tennis court attached and one of the large apartment blocks was vacant undergoing major renovation. The couple of cafes would still be doing business at this time of night in the summer months, but were closed now. The apartment blocks were ornate, pillared numbers. With the rotunda, the area was big on pillars. It wasn't the kind of place where drunks slept on the benches or the homeless camped out with their bags and sheets of plastic. For no good reason, I remembered that the beach had a shark net. Why think of that?

I saw moving shadows now and then and judged them to be swaying tree branches, flickers from occasional car lights, late-night seagulls, flapping bunting left over from some event. The waves were quiet on the beach and rocks, audible but no problem for the microphone. The only other sounds came from passing cars, a distant aeroplane or two, and our breathing.

Headlights. A car drew up on the road adjacent to the rotunda and a man got out. He stared around, squared his shoulders and marched towards the meeting point. Townsend tapped me on the shoulder. His opened hands said, 'Perkins?'

I used the night glasses. I'd only seen the man once, in the Lord of the Isles pub, but there was no mistaking him. He had the belly, the bullying stride. I nodded. Jacques and Townsend did things with their equipment.

Another headlight. Jane Farrow, in jeans and jumper, got out and went towards the rotunda with only the barest glance around. I couldn't decide whether this was a good attitude to take or not. There was enough moonlight to see the two figures as they stood on the steps of the building. I couldn't hear anything, but the body language—a waving hand, a shrug, a vigorous nod—suggested an animated discussion. The sound of Jacques's filming was negligible—a very muted whirr. Townsend stood stock still, his hands clasped in front of him like a penitent.

So far, so good, but I was troubled. Was I right about those shadows? I used the night glasses, swept the field, saw nothing. But there was still a niggle, an irritant. Was it likely that Perkins would come alone? People engaged in dodgy enterprises usually like to have support of some kind.

Weren't there alleged to be two people on the grassy knoll in Dallas? I decided to check on Perkins's car.

Without disturbing the other two, I crouched and retreated, using the shadows of the trees to circle around, go down to the beach, and come up on the cars on the blind side. It was slow going, and moving in a crouch tests muscles you don't always use. No bushman, I had to watch my footing in case there were sticks to snap, rocks to trip over. It took time.

When I was twenty metres from the car I saw movement inside it. The night glasses revealed a figure in the back seat. He touched his left ear several times. Adjusting an earpiece? Then the window slid down and a rifle barrel protruded. Not far, but far enough. The car was fifty metres away from the rotunda with a clear line of sight.

I dropped the glasses and sprinted, stepped around the car, grabbed the barrel and pulled. You don't hold a long firearm tightly; you cradle it. The rifle came free and the man swore. He opened the door and came at me like a charging bull. I hit him hard on the side of the head with the rifle butt. He sagged back against the car but he wasn't done. He lashed out with his foot, hit the rifle and sent it spinning away. The cap he'd been wearing fell off. He was bald, stocky, strongly built. He was my man.

He knew how to fight, coming in low and hard. He was younger and stronger than me, but I had the fuel of rage. He tried a vicious swing at my crotch but I got my knee up in time. The blow hurt, but it hit bone and hurt him more than me. I stamped down hard on his instep and used the leverage to slam my fist into his nose.

That didn't worry him too much and he aimed a kick at my knee. Just missed, and it put him off-balance. I drove a left uppercut into his balls and brought my clenched right fist down on the back of his neck as he dropped. He sprawled on the ground, stunned but still conscious.

I crouched over him like Dempsey over Firpo.

'You killed Lily Truscott.'

He was game, tried to needle me into giving him another opportunity. 'Sure did,' he said, with a flow of blood and mucus running into his mouth. He spat it all up at me. 'Gave her a fucking good feel too, after I did her.'

I pinned him at the throat with my left hand, cutting off his windpipe. I could hear noises around me now—shouts, running footsteps. Torch beams probed the darkness. I didn't care. I reached into my jacket pocket where I'd put the Walther, jerked it free. I hammered my knee into his chest to hold him while I used both hands to cock the pistol. I pressed the muzzle to his forehead.

'Go ahead, cunt. Bet you haven't got the guts.'

I heard a shout, 'Cliff, don't!' *Townsend?*

I pulled the trigger.

26

The gun didn't fire.

Hands grabbed me, arms wrapped around me, and I was dragged away from the man on the ground. Someone tried to take the pistol from me but I chopped the hand down and pushed past people standing in my way. Who were all these people?

I wandered off towards the beach. Someone ran to outflank me but I pointed the pistol at him and he fell back. I went down the steps and across the sand. What I had almost done seemed to put my brain in a spin so that I couldn't see, hear or feel anything until water lapped over my feet and the waves splashed up at me. The shock of the cold water snapped me out of the daze. I drew back my arm and threw the pistol out as far as I could towards the cable holding the shark net and screamed Lily's name as I let it go. It felt like a signing-off of some kind.

They were waiting for me back on the grass. I saw the man I'd flattened being bustled into a car. Townsend was there, and Jacques, and two men I didn't know and two I did—Matthews and Mattioli from Internal Affairs. They kept their distance but I held out empty hands to show them I wasn't armed, just in case they hadn't seen me throw the pistol away.

'What's going on?' I said.

Matthews said, 'You almost committed murder.'

'Didn't though. Who're these other guys? What're you all doing here?'

Jane Farrow came close and touched my arm. 'Thanks, Cliff. I think you saved my life. That guy had a sniper rifle with an infra-red scope, zoned in just right.'

'What do you mean you *think*?' Townsend said.

'She means he might've been going to kill Perkins,' I said. 'With these bastards anything's possible. I still don't understand where everybody's come from.'

'I've been with Internal Affairs all along,' Jane said. 'We knew the unit was dirty and I was working my way to this kind of meeting with someone who'd do a deal against the others. We targeted Gregory, then had to switch to Perkins. Like you, we brought the technicians.'

'But why did you recruit Cliff and me if you already had the plan?' Townsend said, with pain in his normally controlled voice.

A light drizzle started.

'Do we have to do this here?' Mattioli said.

'I didn't trust them,' Jane said. ' After what I've seen the past year or so, d'you blame me?'

It was all a blur of police cars, phone calls and interviews after that. Piecing it together later, I learned that Perkins had made certain admissions, captured on tape and film by both Townsend and Jacques and the Internal Affairs boys. Townsend's results were the better ones.

Perkins implicated Kristos and others in the Northern Crimes Unit and they all started to do the dirty on each other. The man I'd tackled was Paul Henry Brewer, who'd been acquitted on one charge of murder and was suspected of several others. His motorcycle and .22 pistol were located and DNA evidence placed him at the scenes of the murder of Williams and Gregory. Kristos implicated him in the killing of Lily, but he was only charged with the deaths of the two policemen. Stronger cases. I didn't care. I'd heard his admission about Lily and wished I'd hit him a few more times, and harder.

All sorts of charges could have been laid against Townsend—concealing evidence, conspiracy—and me, the same, plus weapons offences. None were. In fact I was almost in good order with the police and they offered me counselling to help me cope with the rage I'd experienced when I'd intended to blow a helpless man's brains out. I told them what they could do with it, politely.

I met with Pam Williams—who'd changed her mind about Sydney—and Hannah Morello after they got back from Queensland. They invited me to a barbecue—kids, in-laws, cousins, family. They thanked me for helping them find some sort of closure with the deaths of their husbands. I thanked them for their contributions in much the same terms. They told me that they'd each received two pieces of legal advice. One suggested that they had cases for compensation from the police service, the other was that their superannuation payments might be in jeopardy if they pursued the matters. Some things never change.

The story made big news for a while but, with the state government struggling in the wake of the resignation of the premier and various bungles, and the federal government in trouble over international embarrassments, politics pushed it aside. But Townsend kept in touch with it and told me that the Northern Crimes Unit business affairs were coming to light and unravelling. The media personality and religious figure turned out to be one and the same—an evangelical church pastor with a TV show. He was found to be black-mailing a church member over a murder with the connivance of the police. He misused substantial federal funds for money laundering ploys involving the cops, and gave confidential information to the police in return for protection by them from complaints as he feathered his nest. This was the main story Lily had evidently been pursuing, but not the only one. Last we heard, the prosecutors hadn't got on to the politician working the immigration scam. Caught some councillors with money and connections they shouldn't have had, though.

Townsend didn't get his inside story. All the evidence was *sub judice*. I stayed in touch with him over the next few weeks as the police and prosecution wheels slowly started to turn. We drank a bit.

'How's Jane?' I asked when we were sipping his single malt whisky on a cloudy day in his neatly bricked courtyard.

He shook his head. 'It didn't work out.'

'Why's that? You did everything she asked.'

'That could've been the problem.'

I knew what he meant. Some women, not that many, want opposition, contest. I said something along those lines.

'Yeah. That's partly it, but she's hooked on the under-cover stuff, the covert, the deceptive. It's like a drug. Remember telling me that there's a gap in her service record?'

'Yeah.'

'She said—don't worry, I didn't let on that you'd told me—that she was doing a course to equip her for under-cover work. She won't surface when all this stuff comes out in the wash. She'll be protected, and she'll be able to go on and do something else under the covers. No pun intended. Shit, I'm pissed.'

'You're human,' I said.

I had a loose end to tie up. I asked Phil Lawton to find out who the IT person for the Northern Crimes Unit was. I had no doubt he could do it and he did, muttering something about systems signatures, whatever that meant. Rodney St Clair, IT consultant with a PhD from MIT, had an office in Chatswood. I made an appointment, claiming to need advice about the installation and servicing of a computer network in my small but growing business.

The office was across the street from the wine bar where I'd met with Lee Townsend and Jane Farrow what now seemed like a long time ago. I promised myself a drink there when I'd finished my business.

St Clair Systems occupied half the building's second floor. It boasted a secretary and several offices. I could hear the clicking of keyboards behind closed doors as the secretary led me to where the boss received his clients. St Clair was a middle-sized man, in his early thirties, neatly groomed. The office was well appointed without being flash. It inspired confidence, but didn't suggest excessive expenditure on overheads. St Clair had risen and come around from behind his desk when I walked in and his hand shot out automatically.

He took one look at me, turned pale and retreated to his chair.

I locked the door behind me and perched on the edge of the desk. I pushed the telephone out of his reach.

'I don't have a small business,' I said, 'and I don't need a consultant. Any buzzers, alarms under the desk?'

'Y … yes.'

'Keep your hands where I can see them. She was still there when you worked on her computer. Lying dead on the bed.'

He closed his eyes as if he was reliving the scene.

'Are you from the police?'

'No. She was my partner.'

'Oh, God …'

'Who else was there? Kristos?'

He nodded, speechless with fear.

I eased back on the threatening manner. 'What did he have on you?'

He struggled to pull himself together. 'What're you going to do to me?'

'Nothing, if I get the information I want. If I don't, you can kiss all this goodbye.'

'I … I installed systems in several businesses and made them less than secure so that Kristos and the others could exploit them. He threatened to expose me if I didn't—'

I stopped him. 'Okay, he had you by the balls. Now, you read what was on her computer, right?'

Nervous again, he nodded.

'What did Kristos want to know? Don't lie to me because I know the answer.'

'He … he wanted to know who in the police had given information to … the journalist … to her.'

'And were you able to tell him that?'

'Yes. There was a code but it was very simple to crack.'

'Who?'

'Someone called Jane Farrow, a detective in the same unit as Kristos.'

I slid off the desk and took a seat while St Clair carefully removed a tissue from a box on the desk and wiped his face.

'You've been lucky,' I said, 'you haven't actually caused anyone's death.'

'I don't understand.'

'You don't have to. You just better hope your name doesn't come up in the investigation of the unit.'

'That's why I was worried when I saw you.'

'Keep worrying.'

I went to the wine bar and ordered a big glass of red. It was late afternoon and getting dark. Could be rain on the way, and I still hadn't done anything about getting the Falcon's wipers fixed. I sipped the wine and thought it through. It made sense in a weird way. Kristos and Perkins knew that Jane Farrow had leaked, but they didn't know she was an Internal Affairs plant. They knew she'd taken kickbacks, as she admitted to Townsend and me—to maintain credibility. They probably thought she was angling for a bigger share of the action or the strategic discrediting of someone blocking her path to promotion. Probably saw her as in league with Williams and took him out to scare her. Then Gregory cracked all on his own and had to be eliminated.

I'd have given a lot to have heard the conversations between Kristos and Perkins after the Internal Affairs people had moved in on the unit after Gregory's death. They must have been sweating. Assuming they still thought Jane Farrow was playing her own game, the chance to kill her when she proposed the meeting with Perkins would have seemed heaven-sent. Brewer was up to the job.

Given the way she'd contributed to Lily's death, and how she'd lied to and manipulated Townsend and me, it was almost comforting to know that she wasn't as clever and covert as she thought she was. Or that things were more complicated than she'd imagined. Almost. Somewhere down the track she might get her comeuppance.

27

Probate on Lily's estate went through smoothly. Tony sold her house and my share was close enough to three hundred thousand. I got another sixty thousand from Lily's share portfolio. I gave a chunk of the money to Megan to help her buy a flat. I spent some on fixing up the Glebe house—the roof, the stairs, the windows. I got new carpets and new bathroom and kitchen fittings. The trees were trimmed, the bricks in the courtyard were re-laid and bits that badly needed it got painted. Plenty of money left over.

I stayed with Frank and Hilde while the work was being done and the strange thing was, when I got back to the house, I didn't like it. Some kind of connection with it had been broken. I junked a lot of the furniture, shoved the rest in storage, put the house up for lease and Frank and Hilde had me back again inside a week.

'So what're you going to do?' Hilde said.

'Ever heard of Tony Truscott?'

'No—oh, well I know the surname ...'

'Lily's younger brother. He's fighting an elimination bout for a shot at the world welterweight title in Nevada next month. He's dedicating the fight to Lily. I'm going over there to support him.'

Frank said, 'Rubbing shoulders with Russ and Jeff and Mike.'

'That's right. Ringside.'

'What then?' Hilde said.

'Travel a bit, I suppose. Europe, the States. I would've liked to have seen New Orleans when it was operating. Might have to settle for Memphis—Graceland, the Sun studios.'

Hilde persisted. 'After that?'

I hadn't looked any further ahead. There were friends scattered around the globe and in Australia. People to catch up with. A few enemies, but no unfinished business.

'Who knows?' I said.

A Cliff Hardy novel by Peter Corris

The Coast Road

Wealthy Frederick Farmer died when his weekender burned to the ground. Death by accident, the police found. But his daughter, Dr Elizabeth Farmer, a feisty academic who resembles the younger Germaine Greer, hires Cliff Hardy to investigate. Is her only motive jealousy of her father's attractive second wife, now very rich?

Hardy's search takes him from the Illawarra escarpment to Wollongong and Port Kembla, and the police are far from co-operative as he tries to unravel the truth. He has his hands full when a panic-stricken call leads to a second case—the search for the precocious daughter of Marisha Karatsky, an exotic, dark-eyed interpreter who gets well and truly under Hardy's guard.

Hardy has narrow escapes and people die as his probing hits nerves. Corrupt cops, compromised insurance agents, feral bikies as well as a few good guys are drawn into the maelstrom. Hardy battles on through personal turmoil and vicious opposition with all outcomes uncertain and justice a remote ideal.

'Hardy has seen off many imitators and lives to drive his beloved Falcon another day.'
The Sunday Age

A Cliff Hardy novel by Peter Corris

The Empty Beach

The early 1980s found Cliff Hardy well established as a private investigator but still battling his demons. He has quit smoking and moderated his drinking. The memory of his brief marriage still haunts him along with other ghosts from his past.

A case in Bondi attracts him as an ex-surfer and admirer of the suburb. It began as a routine investigation into a supposed drowning, but Hardy soon finds himself literally fighting for his life in the murky, violent underworld of Bondi.

The truth about John Singer, black marketeer and poker machine king is out there somewhere—amidst the drug addicts, prostitutes and alcoholics. Hardy's job is to stay alive long enough in that world of easy death to get to the truth.

The truth hurts …

'There has been no more efficient, entertaining and amusing writer of detective thrillers in Australia than Peter Corris.'
The Age

'A fine, tightly controlled story.'
West Australian

A Cliff Hardy novel by Peter Corris

Saving Billie

When journalist Louise Kramer hires Cliff Hardy to find Billie Marchant, Hardy heads for the unfamiliar territory of the far southwestern suburbs of Sydney. Billie claims to have information about media big-wheel Jonas Clement— the subject of an incriminating expose by Kramer. Clement doesn't want Billie found and Clement's enemies want to find her first.

Hardy tracks Billie down, but 'saving Billie' means not only rescuing her, it means saving her from herself. Billie, ex-stripper, sometime hooker and druggie, is a handful. Hardy gets help from members of the Pacific Islander community and others, but the enemies close in and he is soon fighting on several different fronts.

Clement and his chief rival, Barclay Greaves, have heavies in the field, and Hardy has to negotiate his way through their divided loyalties. Some negotiations involve cunning but others involve guns. The action takes place against the backdrop of the Federal election campaign, and all outcomes are uncertain.

'I don't know how many Cliff Hardy novels there are, but there aren't enough.'
Kerry Greenwood, *Sydney Morning Herald*

'Hardy is a wonderful creation still, under Corris's magisterial narrative control, capable of those odd echoes and resonances, the elegiac interludes that characterise the best crime writing.'
Graeme Blundell, *Weekend Australian*